Content Advisory:

S – ENSUOUS
E – ROTIC
X – TREME

Ellora's Cave Publishing offers three levels of Romantica™ reading entertainment: S (S-ensuous), E (E-rotic), and X (X-treme).

The following material contains graphic sexual content meant for mature readers. This story has been rated E–rotic.

S-*ensuous* love scenes are explicit and leave nothing to the imagination.

E-*rotic* love scenes are explicit, leave nothing to the imagination, and are high in volume per the overall word count. E-rated titles might contain material that some readers find objectionable — in other words, almost anything goes, sexually. E-rated titles are the most graphic titles we carry in terms of both sexual language and descriptiveness in these works of literature.

X-*treme* titles differ from E-rated titles only in plot premise and storyline execution. Stories designated with the letter X tend to contain difficult or controversial subject matter not for the faint of heart.

Lord Kir of Oz

ဆ

Dedication

හ

To Bill, Cindy, Ashley, Sammy, Tia, *and* Dusty
One awesome family!

Trademarks Acknowledgment

~

The author acknowledges the trademarked status and trademark owners of the following wordmarks mentioned in this work of fiction:

Mustang: Ford Motor Company
Twilight Zone: CBS Broadcasting, Inc.

Chapter One

ဆ

A tight breath of that *almost-free* feeling pushed from Dorothy Abigail Osborne's chest.

It was time to do it or die.

Aunt Maye was still in town. Before her elderly relative came home, Abby would get ready, shore up her courage and pack her things. She had to get moving before she chickened out again.

Abby marched up the creaking wooden steps of her aunt's farmhouse and flipped her single braid over one shoulder. There was attitude in her gait. She could feel it. Attitude was good. Attitude led to confidence.

Didn't it?

She stopped at the top step. The breath of freedom turned into a hitch in her side.

"Steady," she told herself out loud. "Damn it. I'm not going to freak out. My life is going to change, and by God, it starts today. Right this minute."

Warmth flowed through her veins, hotter than a shot of tequila. Wind tugged at her work shirt, the cool breeze caressing her heated skin, sending a layer of goose bumps tingling across her arms. At breakfast this morning, the TV anchorman warned of a weather change. And sure enough, dark storm clouds rode the horizon.

"Smells like rain."

Breathing freely once more, Abby headed across the wooden porch. Her boots clunked as her lungs filled with the clean, fresh scent of the oncoming storm—along with another odor that made her brows furrow and her nose crinkle. She sniffed once, twice, before casting a downward glance—and stopping in her tracks one more time.

"*Ahhhh, man…*" Pig shit clung to her boots like gum too long in the sun. "Please don't tell me this is a sign of how the rest of my day is gonna go."

Stop it! You're going to psych yourself out.

She felt like the farm was trying to grab hold of her, tell her she belonged where she was, that she was a part of this boring old place and she'd never escape. She wanted to deny it with all of her soul, but damn if she didn't fit right in with all the pungent smells of the barn.

She rolled her eyes skyward. "There's no place like home."

Frowning at the gummy crap trying to ruin her mood, she shook her head. No way would she let a little pig shit take the wind out of her sails. She stomped her boots, wiped them on a nearby throw mat, then gave the mat a good kick across the porch.

A crack of thunder made her jump. She looked up in a hurry. Lord, they were in for one hell of a storm.

The sweet tinkling of wind chimes fought the incoming gale—and brought back a lot of memories. Abby rested her hand on the doorknob, but couldn't make herself go inside. Once she went through that door, the changes would really start. She wouldn't be coming back out a Kansas farm girl.

Slowly, she turned and took one last look at the farm's simple beauty.

Green fields as far as the eye could see spread in either direction. The ancient barn crouched just west of the aging farmhouse where she had grown up. Even the animals grazing in the fields or pecking at the ground gave the farm a sense of hominess.

Motion caught Abby's eye. A flash of red. Her aunt's aging rooster was chasing a leghorn hen around the yard.

In the distance, Bob, the old plow horse, grazed, paying no heed to scraps of newspaper dancing in the air currents around him. She'd never seen her Uncle Henry hitch the horse to the antiquated plow just beyond the barn, but he'd kept the swaybacked animal just in case the "newfangled machine" broke down. That machine—the tractor she'd used for years to till the fields—was behind the big red doors of the barn. In fact, her ass still ached from the hours she'd just spent riding the tractor.

"Enough." Her confidence came flooding back. A sense of independence filled her as she turned to the door.

"Last day feeding chickens, milking cows and slopping the hogs. There's more to life than wooing a stubborn old cow or rounding up a rogue sheep or two."

She'd had enough of animals. The furry four-legged beasts on the farm had seen the last of her. As soon as she took a bath she was heading for New York City. A new city, a new home, and a new beginning.

Abby threw open the door.

The quiet farmhouse greeted her coolly, like it knew she was about to become a deserter.

Whatever.

No more Attica. No more Kansas. No more hog-tying.

Surely her feet would move if she willed it hard enough…

No more men too old, too young or too backwoods.

All she had to do was go inside, get in the shower…

No more relatives who think sex is one of the seven deadly sins. Hell. I'm twenty-five years old. Getting laid on a regular basis by some gorgeous hunk is my God-given right. Make that men. Getting laid by gorgeous hunky men. *As many as possible.*

Finally, she managed to take that big step across the threshold.

"Next living thing I wrestle to the ground'll be tall, dark, handsome, walking on two legs, with a cock long enough to please."

She would find a man who knew how to take care of a woman, knew how to love.

"Uh, I mean men, find plenty of *men*," she amended again, thinking a ménage à trois might be interesting. Maybe a little bondage would be fun. One of her secret fantasies had always been to be tied up and fucked until she couldn't walk straight.

Hell, anything would be interesting compared to the slam-bam-thank-you-ma'ams she'd had so far. It was time to get crazy. Down and dirty.

Yup, Abby had made up her mind and nothing Aunt Maye said would change it. Candlelit nights and satin sheets were only two things on her long list of wishes.

Of course, she had to face her staunch aunt first. Abby's stomach churned. Standing up to Aunt Maye was like standing up to a tornado and praying you wouldn't get sucked up in its fury.

Besides Joey, the kid next door, had promised to help Aunt Maye with the chores. So it wasn't like Abby was leaving Maye to fend for herself.

"What's gotten into me?" She bit down on her bottom lip to silence the feelings of loss. "Suck it up, girl." She had more important things to attend to. She didn't need anybody. From this day forth no one, man or woman, would ever tell Abby what to do.

Thank goodness Aunt Maye's still in town. The screen door squeaked then slammed shut as Abby finally hurried inside the old house that smelled of fresh baked bread, lemon furniture polish and mothballs. The camphor scent clung to everything, including her aunt.

I'll have time to pack, and then once I face her I can hurry on out of here before she turns into a class five twister.

Abby thought about leaving a note and taking off in her little red Mustang, but Aunt Maye and Uncle Henry had taken Abby into their home when she was an infant. She owed her aunt at least a goodbye in person. Maybe it wouldn't be so bad after all.

Yeah, right.

Maye had a good heart, but she kept it hidden behind a sharp tongue and a barbed wire fence. Or at least that's what Uncle Henry had always said before he passed away.

Abby started to head up the stairs only to see Otto, or "O" as she liked to call him, bounding down like the oncoming thunderstorm. She grabbed onto the handrail and waited for the Irish wolfhound to jump up and give her a sloppy dog kiss.

"Yuck, O." Abby wiped dog slobber from her cheek with the back of her hand. "Keep that up and I'll leave you with Aunt Maye." Funny, but she could have sworn the dog shivered before he barked and ran back up the stairs. Abby rolled her eyes and followed after her gangling pet.

Her boots clomped across her bedroom as she hurried to her duffle bag. She threw in her better clothes—the ones that didn't scream she'd been born and raised on a farm. Okay, so she *had* been raised on a farm, but that didn't mean she wanted to look the part.

The ancient bed that had been mended more times than Abby could remember moaned beneath her weight as she plopped herself onto it. She tugged at one disgusting boot and then the other, tossing both simultaneously on top of a pile of unwanted clothes heaped before her closet. Next to follow were her work shirt, jeans, bra, panties and socks.

Abby slipped into the shower, unraveled her braid and shook out the long auburn tresses. Her hair tumbled over her shoulders to brush the small of her back, and she shivered at the thought of a man with gentle hands and lips kissing her there…and everywhere else.

She shampooed her hair with her favorite vanilla-scented shampoo, closing her eyes and imagining that her mystery man was massaging her scalp. The soap that ran from her hair over her breasts and nipples was a sensual caress.

When she'd finished washing her hair, she soaped her body with a gel that matched the scent of her shampoo and lotion. She loved the aroma of vanilla. Her hands paused at her breasts and she tweaked her nipples hard, feeling a burst of pain that eased into pleasure, sending a thrill from her breasts to her pussy.

Lord, what she would give to have a man with her in the shower. She slipped one hand between her thighs and felt how slick she was from her juices. The scent of her arousal rose in the steaming shower and she shivered as her finger pressed against her clit.

In her mind she pictured a sexy man, blond with sapphire eyes that would burn like blue fire. For *her* and her alone. While the warm shower water poured over her, she circled her clit harder. She closed her eyes and pictured his sculpted body, his long, thick cock, his hands on her body.

Yeah, he'd pin her up against the cool shower wall and she'd wrap her legs around his lean hips. He'd drive his cock into her and fuck her. Oh, God, he'd fuck her so hard she'd be crying out for mercy. Screaming with an orgasm that would blow her mind away.

Abby's climax hit her so hard that her body rocked against her hand and her eyes flew open. Still her finger circled her clit, rapid movements, back and forth, continuing to draw out every current zinging through her body, heightening and singeing each nerve ending. Her chest rose and fell with the heaviness of her breathing, and her legs trembled.

Jeez, that had to have been one of the best orgasms she'd ever given herself.

She leaned against the shower glass as the last tingles of sensation dissipated. Her body was warm inside, cooling on the outside, and she loved it. For a moment she thought of going for an encore but time was a-wastin'.

Grabbing a towel off the rack, she stepped from the shower, feeling relaxed and flushed. Abby dried off quickly then brushed out her hair and rebraided it into a single braid. Pussy still tingling, she tugged on a thong, a pair of new jeans, and wiggled into a little spaghetti-strap tank top. Her breasts were small but perky and she didn't have to wear a bra. So her aunt wouldn't have something else to bitch about, Abby quickly threw a denim shirt on over the tank top and tied the ends at her waist.

She grabbed her bottle of vanilla-scented lotion and rubbed it over hands that were dry and callused from all the farm work she was accustomed to doing. Tightening the lid, she tossed the lotion into the bag. The tote's zipper made a hiss as she tugged it closed, then she flung the bag over her shoulder.

Finally, she was ready to go.

With a bounce in her step Abby hurried downstairs, O following close at her heels. First things first. She'd drop the duffle in her car trunk to be ready for a quick getaway once she gave Aunt Maye the news.

And then adios, Attica.

Outside the storm had strengthened. Angry clouds moved rapidly across the sky, twisting, churning, as if someone had placed time on fast-forward. Abby had hoped she'd be down the road by now, before the storm hit. But once again her aunt had foiled her plans.

The bang of a shutter startled Abby as it broke loose from its hinges and slammed against the house. She missed the last step and grappled to catch herself from falling. Only the unsteady porch railing she'd forgotten to fix stopped her from landing flat on her face.

Was even the weather against her leaving this house, this town, this state?

Wind tore at her clothing like a million tiny fingers tugging and pulling her back toward the house. Head down to avoid the rush of air, she determinedly made her way to the car. She wouldn't let Aunt Maye delay her plans, and she wasn't about to let a little weather sway her.

Dust stung her eyes and the taste of dirt was gritty on her tongue as she finally wedged the key into the lock and popped the car's trunk. She tossed in the duffle and struggled to close the trunk while continuing to fight the gust that seemed hell-bent on thwarting her plans. After she slammed the trunk shut with a loud clunk, she smiled and stuffed her keys in her pocket. Now she was just about ready to head off on a new adventure.

"Oh, shit. I forgot to gas up the car." Abby groaned. Hopefully she'd have enough to make it to town and fill it up at the convenience store. But damn it, she'd really pushed it as far down as the gas gauge would go.

As she turned toward the house the wind suddenly died. For a heartbeat all life stilled. Then, slowly, the heavens groaned as if the weight of the world tore at its seams. O whimpered, sinking down on his haunches. His big brown eyes stared up at her. The fine hairs at Abby's nape prickled in warning.

It started as a hollow whistle, building into a thundering noise like an oncoming freight train. The ground shook with the intensity of the rumble coming from behind her.

Abby tossed a look over her shoulder and almost wet her panties. An enormous gray funnel-shaped cloud was just touching down…and it was headed straight for the farm.

For a brief second she stood paralyzed. She thought about running for the storm cellar, but the tornado was too close. Her gaze jerked toward the house, then the car. She'd take the car and hopefully outrun it.

Hands shaking, Abby dug into her pocket and darted around the car. She whipped out her keys and flung open the door, the wind nearly ripping it from her grasp. O bounded into the back seat as Abby slid behind the wheel of her '65 classic Mustang. Her fingers trembled as she jammed the key into the ignition and turned it. She sighed with relief as the engine roared to life.

Without looking back, she floored it and tore down the dirt road away from the menacing twister and away from the only home she had ever known.

Telephone poles looked like toothpicks as she sped past. She was driving fast, too fast. Then from out of nowhere something struck the windshield. Safety glass spider-webbed as the car fishtailed. Pulse racing, she gripped the steering wheel, holding her breath until she forced the car back under control.

Still, the tornado barreled after her. She felt like prey with the devil stalking her.

Visibility was almost nil as dark clouds choked out the sun. The roar was so loud now that Abby couldn't even hear the sound of the car's powerful engine.

Pressure built in her ears. O's hot breath touched the back of her neck. If he hadn't been so close, she wouldn't have heard his whimper.

Abby chanced a look in her rearview mirror to see the tornado consuming everything in its path, the big gray cloud now nipping at her bumper.

She punched the gas, but even as she did she knew it was too late. Dirt and debris surrounded her, blocked her view of the road ahead. In the next moment the car skidded, lost ground and rose, light as a feather.

Abby screamed. O howled.

Her heart crashed against her chest with such force she thought it would explode. What looked like a wooden door sheared off her sideview mirror. She'd never known real fear until now. As the car began to turn, rotate faster and faster, flinging her deeper and deeper into the abyss, bone-numbing terror shook her. Lights, color...her whole world and her whole life flashed by.

Something hard slammed into the back of Abby's head. Bright stars burst behind her eyelids.

So much for getting laid tonight, she thought before everything went black.

Chapter Two

 හ

In his wolf form, Lord Kir loped down the moonlit Yellow Road, away from Emerald City, toward the red beast crouched in the grass beneath a *ch'tok* tree.

Powerful winds unlike anything he had seen in all his many years had brought the monstrosity, then vanished like mist in the woods on a warm summer's eve. He had been on his nightly rounds of his realm when the winds had come out of nowhere. They left behind an amazing rainbow that glittered across the dark sky like stardust and moonlight.

His gaze focused on the red beast. He knew it was not a living being, but that it was a sort of machine — yet nothing like it had ever been found or created in his world. Long before he reached the red object he smelled it — a bitter, acrid odor that nearly clouded his senses. The moon shone bright this night, causing the red beast to glint in the silvery beams.

Kir paused to howl, to affirm his lordship over all within his realm. His cry echoed through his lands from mountain top to mountain top. No one would dare to challenge him — the Alpha male and Lord of the cave-dwelling mountain wolves. He had never been challenged in any way by male or female. He was always obeyed.

His word was law.

Because of the overwhelming stench of the red beast, it wasn't until Kir drew closer that he caught scent of something sweeter. The perfume of vanilla and the smell of rain...and the more intriguing scent of woman — along with the coppery smell of blood.

And the musky odor of another creature…an animal, not unlike a wolf.

Kir slowed his steps as he came upon the red monstrosity that he guessed must be a vehicle of a sort. It had a door flung open.

A beautiful woman sprawled upon the golden pathway at the red beast's feet. She lay completely still, but Kir's senses told him her heartbeat was strong and sure. In the sharp moonlight he saw she had a sprinkling of faerie kisses standing out over the bridge of her nose. Scratches marred her otherwise perfect skin and blood trickled down the side of her face from a cut along her cheek.

Standing over the woman was a wolf-like animal with hackles raised. The creature had a bloody slash across its muzzle. The animal growled and bared its teeth at Kir.

Kir growled in return, bared his fangs, his own fur standing on end. For one moment he thought the creature intended to harm the maiden, but Kir scented the woman's perfume upon the animal and caught the creature's musk on her odd clothing. Likely this animal was her companion.

Relaxing his stance, Kir shifted into his man's form, pelt blending to bare skin, bones popping, shifting and elongating as he rose up to tower over the animal. Even as Kir flexed his powerful muscles, the creature did not back down. Instead it bared its teeth even more and gave a louder growl. Saliva dripped from the animal's mouth and the position of its tail told Kir the creature was willing to attack to protect the woman.

Lord Kir held out his hand, palm facing the animal. He addressed the creature in thought-speech. *I do not wish to harm your mistress,* Kir said in a voice that could control any animal, even if the creature did not understand the words he was saying. *I only wish to tend to her.*

The animal's growl became fainter then slowly died away. His tail lowered. He cocked his head, eyes fixed on Kir, studying him with intelligent eyes. As Kir projected more calming, controlling thoughts, the creature settled on its haunches and looked expectantly at him.

Kir learned from the animal's mind that it was a *dog* and its name was O. It was a descendent of the wolf and a brethren. The woman O guarded was known as Abby.

Kir knelt beside the woman — Abby — and held out his hand to O so that the dog might learn his scent. O sniffed then lowered himself to a resting position, asking Kir with his concerned eyes to tend to his mistress.

With all his focus on the woman now, Kir took one of her hands in his. It felt cold, but her pulse beat steadily. Her skin was roughened as if she was a servant rather than the fair maiden she truly was. Perhaps she had been held prisoner in some faraway land.

Her clothing was certainly odd — like that of a man's, only of different cloth. His cock stirred at the sight of her gaping overtunic. The undershirt was ripped and the lovely swell of one breast was exposed, although her nipple remained hidden from sight. The undershirt had thin straps and was tucked into sturdy blue cloth breeches.

What Abby wore reminded Kir somewhat of the outfits worn by the wives of the Kings of Hearts, Spades, Diamonds and Clubs, before the women had been integrated into this world.

The Kings' women had been from a parallel world called Earth. Could this woman have been brought to Emerald City from the same planet?

Kir brought Abby's hand to his lips and kissed the inside of her wrist. The vanilla scent was stronger. He could feel blood flowing through her veins and heard the beat of her heart. He slipped the fingers of his free hand behind her head and immediately the sticky thickness of blood coated his fingers.

Gods, she had suffered a head wound. How bad he did not know. He would need to get Abby to Emerald City and to the healer at once.

Carefully, he scooped her into his embrace, taking care to not jar her head. When he cradled her in his arms, he held her warm body tight to his bare chest. Her beauty took his breath away. And by the gods—her torn undershirt gaped even more, fully exposing one breast and her taut rosebud nipple.

With a groan he lowered his head and brushed his lips over Abby's, needing some connection with her. When he drew back her eyelids fluttered. He found himself looking into the most beautiful cinnamon eyes he had ever seen.

O whined and placed his paw on Kir's leg. With a dazed, confused look upon her lovely features, she glanced down at the dog. O obliged her by wagging his tail. She turned her gaze back to Kir.

In a soft, husky voice, she murmured, "O, I don't think we're in Kansas anymore."

"No, you are not in Kanzaz," Kir said the unfamiliar word as he studied Abby's finely sculpted features. "You are in my realm," he continued. "I am Lord Kir of the cave-dwelling mountain wolves. I will take you to Emerald City where your wounds will be tended."

"Damn, you're gorgeous." The woman's voice was slightly slurred and she appeared to be trying to focus. "I've always been a sucker for blue eyes and blond hair." Abby placed her hand against his smooth, bare chest and fire licked his body. "For a dream you feel awfully real," she said a second before her eyelids drifted shut and her body went slack.

Kir held the woman carefully as he carried her toward the entrance to Emerald City with O at his heels. Heat raged through his body in ways he did not understand. He had enjoyed the pleasures of many, many women, but he felt such desire for this one, a mad protectiveness he could not fathom.

His bare feet padded along the smooth bricks of the Yellow Road that glittered in the moonlight. It was so named because it was fashioned of gold, a pathway that led from Emerald City to the far reaches of Kir's realm and on to Tarok. Tarok was the name for the lands of the Kings of Hearts, Spades, Diamonds and Clubs. Each King had found his mate and broken the curse of Balin, the King of Malachad.

At the thought of Balin, Kir growled. The bastard now turned his evil intentions toward Kir's realm. Balin had used Mikaela, sister to the Tarok Kings. He had exploited her powers to command the *bakirs* to use powerful mindspells to control the dreams of the people of Tarok and prevent them from conceiving.

King Balin's hold on Mikaela was no more, but his *bakirs* now threatened Emerald City.

In the distance Kir heard the howl of one of his captains, echoed by howls of other members of his forces. The calls of the werewolves assured him that nothing was amiss this night.

Other than the unconscious woman in his arms.

A breeze feathered loose strands of the woman's hair across her face and she stirred in his arms. His cock became a hard ache as she moaned in her unconsciousness and shifted so that her cloth-covered ass rubbed against his mighty erection. Kir gritted his teeth and focused on carrying her to the gates of the city. O never left his side.

Wind brushed Kir's naked body and his long hair rose above his shoulders. Sounds of night birds, the *eloin*, echoed through the evening as they sang from their perches in the *ch'tok* trees. Smells of red starflower blooms met his nose, mingling with Abby's vanilla scent and O's strong musk.

When he reached the golden gates to Emerald City, the wolf guards shifted into men and bowed to Lord Kir. He nodded to each of them, Las and Jaco. Although a hint of surprise registered in the guards' eyes at the sight of Abby and O, both were the finest caliber of warriors and made no other sign that anything unusual had happened. Not one of his people would question their leader without his permission.

And he was not inclined to speak of this woman until he knew more about her. And why she had ended up in his realm.

Once the warriors opened the gate, Kir carried Abby into Emerald City. A feeling of pride welled up in his chest and he wished she could see his city at this very moment. He had entered the main cavern, fashioned by nature out of emeralds of all shapes and sizes. They were always lit from the glowing lichen that grew around the base of each emerald.

His people made their way through the cavern either as naked humans or in their wolf forms. There were many couples enjoying one another's pleasures in pools and upon natural moss beds surrounded by fragrant underground blossoms. Yes, his was a magnificent city.

At the far end of the cavern, a rushing waterfall tumbled into an enormous pool surrounded by blooms of red, yellow, purple and orange, which glowed in the light of the emeralds. It was a beautiful place and he found himself looking forward to sharing it with this woman.

Kir shook his head. What strange thoughts were these?

All he should be concerned with was taking her to the healer and attending to her wounds. He felt the stickiness of the blood from her head injury against his biceps and was concerned that the wound was still bleeding.

O constantly kept on the lookout as if trusting no one but Kir with his mistress.

When he reached the diamond chamber, he approached Linara, the dark-haired and lovely healer. She was naked, as his people normally chose to be when not in their wolf forms. Usually the sight of her large breasts, berry-red nipples and the dark curls between her thighs created a raging lust that demanded satisfaction. But today he felt only concern for this Abby, who had virtually fallen from the sky to land in his arms.

His need for Abby was odd and powerful—as was his sense of protectiveness, not to mention the intensity of his attraction to her. A different sort of longing spread through him, strange and new. As if he would know no satisfaction but what she might give him. As if he would have none but her henceforth.

Ridiculous. I must be tired from the hunt.

"Who is this human, M'Lord? And the beast?" Linara set down the amber vial she had been holding and moved toward Kir and Abby. She gestured toward one of the beds occupying the healer's room. "Please set her there."

"Her name is Abby and the creature is called O." Kir gently laid Abby upon the soft bed on her side to allow the healer access to the back of the woman's head. "She is injured and needs our assistance."

"Of course." Linara bowed respectfully, her onyx and silver necklace glinting in the light from the glowing diamonds in the room. She took a cloth from one of the counters built from black stone and diamonds, then moved toward a small hot spring in one corner and dipped the cloth into the steaming, healing waters. "A lot of blood," she said when she returned. "Let us hope she has not bled too much."

Linara took the cloth and gently wiped the sticky fluid and debris from the back of Abby's head. She stirred and moaned. O whined. Kir rested his hand on Abby's arm, squeezing it gently, hoping to comfort her.

The entire time, the huge dog watched and kept one paw on the bed, as if making sure his mistress was being well cared for.

Linara unraveled Abby's braid, releasing her beautiful hair. Her skin was pale and creamy against the dark red of her tresses.

After Linara cleansed away the worst of the blood and dirt, the healer ran her palms above Abby's slim body, from her head to her toes. A silver glow spilled from the healer's hands, enveloping Abby.

Linara closed her eyes. "No broken bones. She is not bleeding within. Beneath her clothing she is bruised and she has several cuts. The worst injury is to the back of her head." The healer opened her eyes. "Her skull is fractured. She needs the full power of the healing springs."

Kir's gut churned at the news of her injury. But certainly the healing springs would mend the wound in little time. Linara and Kir carefully stripped Abby of her bloody clothing. They slipped the overshirt from her arms, then Kir ripped the minuscule undershirt from her chest, fully revealing her small, firm breasts.

He nearly groaned aloud.

When they finished undressing Abby, Kir scooped her into his arms. Abby's naked body felt warm and sensual against his and he bit the inside of his cheek, trying to check the lust raging through him.

"Would you like my assistance, M'Lord?" Linara asked, her gaze darting to his obvious erection.

Kir gave a dismissive nod. "I will tend to the woman."

"I will care for the animal then." The healer bowed and turned to O.

O started to follow Kir but Kir put up his hand. *Go with Linara,* Kir commanded. *I will return with Abby when she is healed.*

The dog whined but settled on his belly, his bleeding muzzle on his forelegs, his large brown eyes staring up at Kir and Abby. Kir gave another brief admonition then moved away. He was certain Linara would care for the dog's injury while he tended to Abby.

Kir turned and rounded the corner, passing a thick black and diamond column that sparkled with the natural glow of the lichen, and entered a private chamber.

Steam wafted from the larger healing pool, the smell of sulfur mingling with Abby's sweet scent. A sheen of perspiration covered their skin. Snowy white sand shifted beneath his feet as he walked over a small bank and into the pool. Sweat formed at his temples and the warm waters caressed his skin.

As he lowered himself onto one of the carved stone benches, Abby gave a soft sigh and snuggled closer, her nice round bottom firm against his cock. Kir did groan aloud this time.

He tipped her head back so that the amoeba in the pool could begin mending the wounds to her head. He carefully held her, supporting her by her neck so that her face remained above water. He gently washed the remains of blood from her hair while the silken strands caressed his hands and his thighs. He felt the amoeba tingling against his hands, searching for any injuries they could find.

Kir studied Abby's features. Her pale, cream-colored skin, her eyelashes that were dark crescents against her pale flesh, that sprinkling of faerie kisses across the bridge of her nose. But what surprised him more were those scattered over her shoulders. He had never seen so many upon a woman before and he found it incredibly arousing. He imagined what it would be like to run his tongue over each and every one of those faerie kisses. To explore her body from head to toe with his mouth and hands.

His eyes slowly perused her from her fae features to the elegant curve of her neck. His gaze lingered on her small, firm breasts and taut, rosebud nipples. He continued down to where the blue-green water lapped over her tiny waist, her slim hips and the auburn curls between her thighs. As if he couldn't help himself, he moved his fingers to her mons and gently tangled his fingers in her curls.

Her thighs were firm and slim, her calves strong and sexy. She was simply succulent. He watched as the amoeba knitted together the cuts on her calves, her thighs, her belly, leaving only pale lines. Her bruises vanished and soon her skin was almost perfect again. He felt the back of her head and was relieved to feel that the amoeba were doing their job and fixing the wound upon her scalp.

As he examined her naked body, a vivid fantasy came to him. Of making her his. Showing her that he possessed her, that she belonged to him. How her lips would feel upon his cock, taking him deep while he thrust in and out of her mouth, her hands bound behind her. And gods, what it would feel like to plunge into her wet quim and fuck her until she screamed.

His gaze returned to her face and his heart stuttered when he saw her lovely cinnamon eyes focused on him.

"Wow," she said with amazement in her voice. "So this is what it's like to die and go to heaven."

Chapter Three

ॐ

It was another one of Abby's perfect dreams. A man sculpted from the very hands of God held her suspended at the water's surface, one palm at the nape of her neck, the other nestled in her lower curls, a breath away from her swelling clit. She squirmed. If he'd just move an inch and run his finger over the target, she'd explode.

They locked gazes, his somewhat surprised, hers pleased — if not ecstatic — at this incredible dream.

The most delicious tremor raced up her spine as her nipples tightened.

She couldn't resist reaching up and running her fingers through the dream man's golden blond hair. It cascaded past his shoulders. So soft. So silky.

She tugged on the tawny strands, guiding his head downward, closer to hers. He didn't resist, nor did he need any encouragement to press his lips to hers.

The kiss was light, tentative, an act of discovery — but it was too fast, too brief. Dismayed, Abby let her eyes flutter open. This time the vivid blue gaze that met hers was carnal and demanding.

The man growled. He actually *growled* before he captured her mouth in a hungry assault.

Hot damn! Now this was a kiss.

With a firm and commanding movement, he thrust his tongue between her parted lips. The pressure at the back of her neck increased as he deepened the kiss, ravishing her, sucking hard and drawing her tongue into his mouth.

He tasted hot and untamed, like a warm breeze on a summer's moonlit night. He even smelled of freedom, an earthy, woodsy scent, as if he had been created from the earth itself. The aroma of pine mingled with something she couldn't identify, which added a hint of mystery.

The heat of the water, the sultry air and the gorgeous man's kiss made Abby's blood boil and her body scream for more.

She moaned, loving the feel of his invasion, but it was nothing compared to the moment his finger slipped between her thighs and plunged into her pussy. She bucked against his palm. He pressed harder, deeper. The rough texture of his skin scraped across her flesh and intensified the sensation, sending bolts of pleasure up her core. Another finger pressed deep inside her as his thumb stroked her clit, setting her into motion.

Abby's hips rose and fell to the rhythmic beat of water lapping against the embankment. Again, her dream man released a sexy growl against her mouth that urged her to ride his hand harder and faster. Her inner muscles clenched around the fingers buried in her channel.

Her orgasm stormed and then shattered her entire being. No warning, no subtle build-up. Just a tidal wave of heat and sensation washing through her body. She screamed, jerking against the violent tremors.

Her mystical dream lover tore his lips from hers, his eyes dark with desire. Before the aftershocks of her climax subsided, she found herself wrapped in his arms as he carried her to the moss-covered bank. His jaws were clenched. His breathing labored. He gently laid her on the mossy green carpet then followed her down and stretched across her.

In her dream she noticed there were two pools of water, including the one where she'd had that incredible orgasm.

Both were so clear she could see the bottom. A cloud of steam rose from the surface and the faint scent of sulfur filled the air. Several black and diamond-like columns sparkled as if small lights had been embedded in the stone. Flowers of every shape, size and color sprang from crevasses in the cave walls, with glimmering moss dangling beneath them. The sand beside the pool was white. It reminded her a little of Christmas, when colored lights burned brightly and the land was coated with a blanket of snow.

And the dream man above her—he was magnificent as his body pressed against hers.

Slowly her fingertips grazed his strong aristocratic jaw and the square chin that held all the qualities of nobility. Pride and strength was carved into his features. Even without clothing he had the presence of a king.

He was the very essence of…well, perfection.

In fact, the Adonis was almost too perfect. And in Abby's experience anything that appeared perfect had to have at least one hidden flaw, maybe more.

But this was her dream man. If her subconscious wanted perfection, then she would damn well take perfection.

And he was all hers to do with as she wished.

Yummy.

Her palm slid over his smooth, tanned skin that stretched taut over rippling muscles and rock-hard abs. Her gaze drank in all that delicious flesh just past his bellybutton to where they touched.

And what was that long, thick piece of heaven pressing into her thigh?

Mmmm… If all dreams were this realistic, she'd never want to wake up. Mister Sandman had worked overtime to create this man out of her hopes, dreams and imagination.

The most incredible sense of serenity seeped deep into her body. Slowly, she bent her arms, stretched and released a heavy sigh of contentment. Intense blue eyes followed her every movement. The dream man didn't make a sound.

She'd heard him growl, so he wasn't mute. And she knew he wasn't a eunuch, because of that cock firmly pressed into her hip, which she had every intention of having between her thighs.

A giggle bubbled up inside her, just before she heard a female voice followed by a loud bark.

"M'Lord."

The man's intense gaze snapped up and over to an arched doorway. At the same time, Abby followed his gaze to see O pulling against a leash held by a dark-haired woman—a woman so lovely that it made Abby pause. The fact that the woman was buck naked except for an onyx and silver necklace around her slender throat made Abby wonder where this dream was headed.

"Linara, you have displeased me." Abby's dream man's annoyance rumbled low and alarming through her body wherever they touched. She felt him tense. Abby reached for him but he didn't pay attention to her. His fiery gaze was pinned on the dark-haired woman.

The woman he referred to as Linara bowed her head. "Yes, M'Lord. However, the beast would not obey. He wishes to be with his mistress."

What a surprise, they were having problems with O. *Not.* Abby wanted to laugh, but the stern look on the man's face suffocated her amusement.

"Linara, I will punish you for this interruption."

Abby's eyes widened as her perfect dream lover threatened the naked woman.

Linara's gaze dropped to the ground. "As you wish, M'Lord." Her voice cracked.

Abby's fantasy man rose, leaving her sprawled on the ground. She pressed her palms on the moss and started to rise.

This dream was getting out of control fast. She had half a mind to order her dream lover back to her.

As if hearing the thought, the man paused, narrowed his eyes and frowned. "Remain where you are, wench, or you will be next in line for punishment."

Abby's eyebrows shot up. She felt like they almost met her hairline. "What the fuck? I think I liked you better when you didn't speak."

"You have earned your first punishment." His tone was harsh. He turned dismissively and without another word approached the submissive, dark-haired woman.

Two men appeared out of thin air behind Linara. Both of them were in the same state of undress and had erections that made Abby lick her lips. Oh, Lord, now this dream was getting *good* again.

The dark-haired man crossed his arms over his broad chest. "You beckoned us, M'Lord?"

"Lan and Eral, kneel facing each other." From out of nowhere, an eight-pronged leather strap appeared in dream man's hand.

Abby's eyes widened. *Oh my god*, he planned to flog the woman. What friggin' path was this crazy dream headed down? Maybe she should wake up.

But then she'd miss what happened next…

It was just a dream. What could it hurt to watch? It might even be a little juicy. Abby squeezed her legs together to calm her clit. What the hell. It wasn't like she'd get to experience this in real life anytime soon.

Linara's head remained bowed, her hands behind her back and her feet positioned apart. O's leash had slipped from her palm but the dog remained beside her, just staring at the man issuing orders like he was King Tut.

A light sheen of sweat glistened on the woman's flesh from the sultry air—or was it from fear? Heavy, deep breaths caused Linara's chest to rise and fall even more rapidly. At the sight of her large breasts, the two kneeling men glanced at one another and smiled. Lust burned hot in their eyes.

"Lan, heads or tails?" Abby's dream man asked the dark-haired guy with biceps as large as one of Abby's thighs. The man must be a helluva weightlifter to have carved his muscles into such a dramatic state of definition. He was almost four inches shorter than Abby's man, but around six feet nonetheless, and definitely impressive.

Amazingly, the man's thick cock grew harder and longer. "Heads." His copper eyes gleamed like shiny new pennies as he wet his lips.

"Eral, your pleasure?" This time he addressed the silver-haired man with sky blue eyes. The man couldn't be older than his late twenties, yet his hair was as lustrous as if it had been spun with silvery thread. In fact, there was something mystical in the man's quiet demeanor—as if he was part Elvin mixed with some Viking. Although he appeared amiable, Abby figured that no man in his right mind would dare screw with him.

"I like it tight." The man's husky response revealed his eagerness. His hot gaze caressed the dark-haired woman's ass.

What kind of game was this?

Then it hit Abby like a baseball bat to the head. These men were going to fuck Linara at the same time while Abby's now ex-dream man flogged the woman.

Abby's wide-eyed stare went from one man to the other and then to the woman. Linara's lowered eyes appeared to glaze over...with what? Fear?

Oh my god, it's excitement. There was a hint of a smile on Linara's lips as her tongue slid seductively over her mouth.

"Linara, on your hands and knees between Lan and Eral," the oh-so-*not*-perfect man commanded.

The woman obeyed without hesitation, sliding between the two men so that her face was level with muscleman's swollen cock, while her ass was inches away from Snow White's rock-hard erection. Snow White bent and lapped several times at her slit. The woman's elbows gave as a tremor shook her body. She fought to gain the strength to pull herself up.

"You have earned another punishment," barked the man Abby wasn't so impressed with anymore. However, the expression of ecstasy on Snow White's face as he licked his lips made Abby spread her thighs a little wider. Her fingers ached to stroke her swollen folds, to pinch and tease her clit, or better yet—to feel her not-so-Mr. Wonderful's cock buried deep inside her.

So he was an ass. This was a dream. She could use him for what he was worth, couldn't she?

"Take Lan into your mouth. And remember, Linara, if you come without permission you will be punished." Abby shivered at his words. One, how the hell was the woman going to resist the climax of her life while being fucked by two gorgeous men? And two, Abby didn't like the sound of anyone being punished.

Lan grabbed a fistful of the woman's ebony hair, jerking her head up so that her neck arched and strained against her necklace. "Watch me, wench, while I fuck your beautiful mouth." Her glazed gray eyes locked with his as she slowly drew her lips over his engorged cock. In a gentle rhythm she began to suck the man's staff. The man clenched his jaw as his strokes went shallow, then deep, deep.

Abby watched her dream apparition raise his hand.

The whip popped before it landed on the tender skin of the woman's shoulder. Her cry was muffled around Lan's cock as he continued to thrust in and out of her mouth.

"Silence." A flick of his wrist and leather stung the woman's other shoulder. This time she didn't make a sound. Faint pink marks rose along her pale skin.

Abby pressed a palm to her mouth to restrain sounds of fear and excitement that nearly choked her.

"Eral," the former dream man said before he lashed out at the woman, this time marking her butt cheek.

A feral grin made Eral's eyes glow as he slathered his cock with a gel.

Now where the hell did that stone jar come from? wondered Abby. And then, poof! Right before her eyes the container disappeared. Okay, it *was* a dream. Anything was possible.

Eral's large hands gripped Linara's hips. "So sweet and tight," the man purred as he placed his erection at the woman's anus. He playfully poked at Linara's rosebud. Her watery eyes grew wide, wider as he teased her. But by the lift of her ass, the way she leaned into his cock, Abby knew the woman was breathlessly awaiting the moment of invasion, of fullness, of being fucked by this mysterious man.

Shit, who wouldn't want that kind of pleasure?

The look of rapture on Eral's face as he thrust into Linara's ass was enough to weaken Abby's knees. She would have fallen if she hadn't already been sitting.

A gasp caught in Abby's throat. In disbelief she watched the woman being screwed from both ends. One man held her head, fucking her mouth. The other held her hips as he pumped in and out of her ass.

When another lash landed on the woman's butt, Abby felt the hot, wet heat of her arousal slide down her thighs. Even the whipping was turning her on.

Fact was, Abby wanted to join the party of four and it scared her. Scared her shitless. Thank God it was just a dream.

She watched as Linara's limbs began to quiver, then stared as the quiver overtook her body. Linara's eyes were fully dilated as she refused to break the locked stare she and Lan held. She squirmed. Amazingly, she fought off her obvious need to climax. Abby's respect for the woman grew. Linara had a constitution of steel to hold back her orgasm like that.

Abby wasn't as strong. Her hand slid between her thighs, but the feral look on *M'Lord's* face stopped her cold.

"Do not touch yourself," he commanded. "You have not earned the right of pleasure."

Aroused and flushed with embarrassment at being caught masturbating, Abby jumped to her feet. "Fuck this. Dream or no dream, I'm out of here. Where's the nearest exit from La-La Land?" Yet before she could take a step she found herself locked tight in the man's arms. His warm breath flooded over her face. "Whoa, this is some freaky stuff. I didn't even see you move."

"Silence," he growled, "or you will feel the sting of my strap."

Ummm…she'd rather feel the sting of his engorged cock in her pussy. The member currently jabbed painfully at her stomach. She couldn't help giving a little wiggle, couldn't stop herself from snuggling up to his erection.

He raised a brow, but looked away as Lan howled and ejaculated in Linara's mouth. As the man pumped while pulling at the woman's hair, her throat moved up and down, swallowing his seed. Then Eral thrust hard with his own climax, forcing Linara forward, causing Lan's cock to ram deeper down her throat. She choked, struggled to breathe as tears fell onto her flushed cheeks. Eral raised his face to the ceiling, his cry of ecstasy almost musical.

Linara trembled as Lan pulled his cock from her mouth and Eral slipped from her ass. She clenched her eyelids, fighting her body's needs. Every muscle was tense. She shook, as if at any moment she would shatter into a million pieces.

"Linara, you may come now," came dream man's deep voice.

Instantly the woman arched. She cried out with relief as she climaxed at her lord's command.

Abby was spellbound. Was it an illusion, or could she actually see the woman's orgasm move beneath her pale skin?

Abby blinked hard and then again. The woman's flesh was rippling and changing colors. In a heartbeat her ivory skin flashed blue, green, yellow and magenta.

Now that's an orgasm of a different color.

This dream was getting too weird. "Wake up, Abby. Please wake up." She would just pinch herself and then she'd wake up. But when she raised her hands she found both wrists bound together by a silk rope.

Shock, fear and then anger exploded inside her. "Let me go." She glared at the son of a bitch, wondering just how he'd managed to bind her.

The golden-haired man's arms crossed his broad chest. His stance was wide and there was a twinkle of laughter in his deep blue eyes. "You landed within my realm; therefore, you are my property."

Abby's jaw dropped. Quickly she regained her composure. "Think again, *asshole*. I'm no man's property, least of all yours." She raised her wrists. "Now take this rope off me."

The arrogant man smirked.

"I liked you better when you didn't speak *or* smirk." Abby shook her head. "You sure know how to screw up a girl's wet dream."

Muttering to herself about her out-of-control subconscious, she managed to push herself to her knees and turn away from him. She intended to find some way to wake herself. Right now.

When a lash landed across the cheeks of her ass, her entire body jerked in surprise. A scream ripped from her throat and she almost tumbled face-first onto the moss.

There wasn't pain in a dream. Yet, did her ass ever sting.

She tried to lunge to her feet but a strong hand jerked her back. Fists clenched, she swung her bound hands toward the man and fought him as if her life depended on it. And it just might. He was going to beat her—maybe even kill her.

Kicking and screaming, she cried, "Let me go—let me go—let me go!"

"Calm yourself, wench," the arrogant man demanded, grasping both her upper arms so tightly she couldn't move.

O growled, wedging himself defiantly between Abby and the man holding her prisoner. The dog growled once more in warning. Abby's heart pounded against her chest. Still she tried to comfort O, placing her tied hands palms-down on his head.

When Abby could finally speak, she said, "This isn't a dream, is it, O?" She glanced at the dog, looking for confirmation as if she expected him to respond. Her mind turned slow circles around the truth. She felt dizzy and giddy. Terrified and intrigued. Was she losing her mind? She had to be losing her mind. Places like this…this twisted sexual Wonderland didn't really exist.

Did they?

She raised her gaze to her captor.

Oh, shit.

His feral stare was as real as real could get.

Her chest actually hurt. The slow circles in her mind stopped abruptly, and her survival instinct took over.

Fine. Just…fine.

So she had gotten herself trapped in some sort of fucked-up fairy tale. She could get herself untrapped. And if she was going to get out of the place, free of this man, she needed to keep her senses about her, she needed to calm down. Buy time. Get a little information.

"What do you mean I 'landed' in your realm?" she asked as carefully as she could.

"Powerful winds delivered you." M'Lord released her arms and she saw he still grasped the flogger in one big hand. "You arrived inside a smelly red chariot."

The tornado, her car…

Oh, God. Okay, so this really wasn't a dream. But it probably wasn't Wonderland either. Somehow she had survived the tornado and been flung into some freaky-ass cult.

Shit! The tornado must have blown her clear to Tennessee. Way back in the hills. Where no sane person would ever, ever find her again.

And if this could happen to her, what about Aunt Maye? What about Bob, locked in the pasture, and that damned horny rooster? What about the farm, the barn? Was Aunt Maye okay?

So much for calming down.

"Who are you?" she demanded. "Where the hell am I? And what have you done to my car?" She heard her voice getting higher and louder with each question, but she couldn't stop herself.

"I am Lord Kir." The man opened his arms wide but all she could see was his broad chest. "And this is Emerald City, my kingdom."

"Yeah." She released a sharp breath. "And I'm Dorothy and this is Toto." She gathered up O's leash. "Don't play stupid with me. Where's my Mustang?"

When the man only glared at her, she said, "Forget it. Where are my clothes? I need a telephone."

While she'd drifted through what she thought was a dream, her nakedness hadn't bothered her. But it sure bothered her now, even if the other four people present were just as naked.

"You're mine to do with as I wish." M'lord spoke as if kidnapping and slavery were an everyday occurrence.

Hell. This was the boonies and he was clearly a nutcase.

Abby leaned slightly forward, her palms still resting on O's head. "*Newsflash*! Slavery was outlawed years ago. It's the twenty-first century, or hasn't anyone let you in on that little secret?"

He reached for her.

She jerked away from his hand. "Touch me and I'll sue your ass."

"I am Lord of the mountain-dwelling cave wolves." His shoulders seemed to broaden, his chest grow more muscular. "You have much to learn if you are to be happy in Emerald City."

Abby released an exasperated breath. "You're friggin' nuts if you think I'll live like a mole and be a slave to an arrogant pretty boy. Come on, O, let's get out of here."

Despite her words, she doubted any mole had ever lived like this. There was something sensual and mysterious about this place. She just wouldn't give that bastard the satisfaction of admitting it.

As Abby turned to leave, her exit was blocked by Lan and Eral. "Move it, boys." Her voice was firm but the men didn't budge. "I said move, if you value your family jewels!"

The next thing Abby knew, the two men each had her by an arm and they were leading her down a narrow corridor. At first she could only stumble forward in shock, but then she began fighting against their hold with everything she had.

They didn't so much as flinch. Abby kicked. She tried to punch. Nothing worked. Jewel-encrusted walls flashed by as they marched her down the path. Diamonds, rubies, sapphires, opals—a wealth of gems scattered everywhere. What she wouldn't give for a pick-ax and bag to carry her treasures.

Well, after she conked the giant-dicked bastards over the head.

The neon green light glowing from the emeralds seemed to dim the farther they went, until they came to an archway lined with black onyx. As the men pushed her through the doorway, Abby gasped. The room looked like it had been used for torture back in the thirteenth century. Whips, chains and strange contraptions—she could only imagine their use—hung from the walls. The walls themselves were gray and stone cold. Even the floor appeared inhospitable. The carpet of moss was gone—only rough, hard rock scraped against her feet. Clearly this cavern was not meant to make a girl feel at home.

Fear slithered through her. But it was nothing compared to the ice cold terror that froze her when Lan raised her hands, lifted her a bit and draped her bindings over a silver hook suspended in midair. Her pulse raced. Her heart slammed hard against her chest as she pushed to her tiptoes to relieve the pressure on her wrists.

"Leave us," Lord Kir ordered as he entered the dungeon-cave and approached Abby.

The two hench-dicks bowed and left the chamber.

All Abby could do was clench her fists and breathe hard. She was totally helpless, naked, stretched out for Lord Kir's examination.

And did he ever examine. His eyes stroked her naked body like a lover's touch. He seemed to be looking for something—but what? Arousal? Abby's desire to fall at his feet and beg for an orgasm?

Well, fuck him—and not literally. She hated the son of a bitch and she let her eyes and expression speak for her.

Still, he kept looking. Kept caressing her with those fire-hot eyes.

Her nipples beaded, and the moisture between her thighs grew hot and wet under his scrutiny.

After a few unbearably quiet moments, he took a deep breath and murmured, "Beautiful." Then he stepped forward, lowered his head and flicked his tongue against her nipple in a light swipe.

A tremor shook Abby. She swore at her reaction, and the bastard actually smiled.

"Man, how I'd like to knock that grin right off your fucking face," she growled through clenched teeth.

"You deny your own desires." He took both of her breasts in his palms and lightly kneaded them. "So be it. I will give you time to consider your words and deeds, to come to accept my touch and to accept me as your lord."

She released an *in-your-dreams-pal* huff.

He pressed his lips to hers. She refused his probing tongue until he pinched one of her nipples so hard that she gasped. Then he invaded her mouth with one thrust.

A moan betrayed her defiance. Again, she felt a sense of freedom in his kiss, his touch. When their mouths parted, her eyes remained closed, waiting for more.

"I will return," he whispered in her ear. "When I choose to do so."

Abby's eyes popped wide, but he was already gone. Not just leaving through the door, but gone. The last thing she saw was a golden tail swish before it disappeared beyond the open door. At first she thought it was O, but her dog lay quietly nearby, watching her from across the room. And besides, O wasn't golden.

"I will return when I choose to do so," she snarled after Lord Kir. "Whatever, asshole. I won't be here!"

No answer.

Okay, okay. Don't waste energy. Think this through. Abby relaxed against her bonds and began to fiddle with the bulging knot binding her. She was tired, overwhelmed and confused. Not to mention pissed. The son of a bitch had tied her up like a pig to market and left her to stew. But he hadn't counted on Abby's ability with knots, knots of any kind. Hell, she could tie and unravel a half crown, even a diamond or clove hitch. You didn't work on a farm with stubborn animals and not know how to handle a rope or the messes a cow, goat or horse could get into.

The arrogant man had used a simple figure-eight. She'd be out of here in no time.

Like right now.

As she pulled the last of the knot free, she lowered her arms and rubbed her wrists. Jerk. That hadn't been too comfortable. She'd get *Lord* Kir for that in court. Had to be worth another year in prison, at least.

Glaring in the general direction Lord Kir had gone, she whistled. "Come on, O."

The dog jumped to his feet, wagging his tail as she reached the door. She scratched the top of his head. "All right. You use that incredible nose, boy. I'm counting on you to get us out of here and back to the car."

He yipped and then sat down. His defiant stance made Abby pause.

"O," she said firmly, "you'd better get your ass up and in gear or I'll have you neutered the first chance I get."

The dog jumped to his feet and rushed passed her.

"That's better." Abby took one look around, stepped through the doorway, then smiled. "Adios, *Lord* Kir."

Chapter Four

ဢ

A flowing white robe swirled around Balin's ankles as he stormed down the corridor. His footsteps pounded out his anger as he shoved a man out of his way. The innocent servant skidded across the polished marble floor until he slammed into the wall with a *thud*.

The sound gave Balin cold comfort. His *bakirs* had failed yet again.

The auburn-haired woman who fell from the sky had been within his reach!

The King of Malachad clenched his fists. Talons sharpened with fury and bit into skin. Tears of blood surfaced on his palms. "Someone will pay for this humiliation." A humiliation he felt straight to his bones.

The door between the realms was easy enough to open, but he had tapped on his reserve magic and that of his unsuspecting people to locate the woman and then create the storm that brought her to his world. He shuddered with fury. The heat of his anger flushed across his face. The strain had left him weak. A feeling he abhorred. One he would never admit to.

His footsteps hastened, his robe swiping against his legs with each step.

A maiden walking toward him took one look and ducked into an alcove. Bella, he thought her name was. She wasn't quick enough.

He grabbed her by the arm, dragging her as he continued down the hall.

She didn't fight him. There was no use in that. The maiden had been taught what all of Balin's subjects learned at an early age—their master would have what he wanted.

And right now he wanted a whipping boy...or girl.

In his mind's eye he pictured the moment when his crystal ball had revealed to him his adversary's mate. In recent days Balin had felt the disturbance in the air, the emptiness in the wolf's cries, a need the arrogant man had not yet understood. In an attempt to get to the woman before Kir, Balin had sent his enchantments over his world and that of the Kings, then through the doors of other worlds in search of Kir's mate.

He had almost had her within his grasp. His fist clenched tighter. She was the key to the wolf's destruction, the man's soulmate, his other half. Without her Kir would slowly lose grip on his control—his state of balance thrown into disarray.

Balin's footsteps slowed as he reached his chambers. He released the young woman as he swung open the door and waved her forward. "You will submit to me freely?"

She bowed her head, took the stance of a slave, legs parted, hands clasped behind her. "Yes, Sire. Of course, Sire."

His nostrils flared as he ravished Bella with his hard gaze. He had hoped to be sampling Lord Kir's woman at this moment.

Bella's eager assent relaxed him a fraction—but not much. Only his iron resolve kept him from turning the full fire of his rage on the brunette in front of him.

Yes. He needed to rein himself in. Scarring her would be such a pity. Those long, shapely legs, that tiny, nipped-in waist—and the full, firm breasts. This was a slave to be savored, not damaged.

His cock thickened and pressed against the silk of his robe. The cool material slid over his heated member and made him harden even more.

"Strip," he commanded. "Slowly."

Before the woman even moved, he parted his robe and cupped himself in anticipation. His hand glided from balls to crown.

The woman before him was new to his kingdom. She would be a good diversion until his captain returned to Malachad with news of why his plan to capture the redheaded woman had failed.

As he fondled himself, the woman drew her arm out of the sleeveless shirt, exposing golden skin inch by inch.

Good, good. Already someone had begun her training. By his command, all women in Malachad were taught how to pleasure him, for they were his playthings by right and station. Oh, yes. He was King of Malachad—and soon to be the ruler of Emerald City as well.

If his thrice-damned *bakirs* could manage a few strategic victories.

The recent failure of his men made him tighten his hold on his cock. Pain shot through his groin—sweet and welcomed. Only the sensual movements of the woman's svelte body as she revealed one breast and then the other forced him to release his hold.

He took a step forward. "Enough."

She halted upon his command.

His index finger extended and the nail began to grow, thinner and sharper, until a hooked claw formed completely. Another three steps had them face to face. She was shorter than his six feet two inches, coming only to his shoulders.

With his talon, he sliced the material of her tunic down the middle. It floated over her arms and to the stone floor.

His heated gaze took in her dusky pink nipples before he reached for the material wrapped around her waist. As his fingernail came closer to her tender skin, she inhaled, leaving a safe gap between her flesh and the cloth. Balin inserted his talon and cut the garment from her body. Then his fingernail retracted and reshaped in human form once more.

She trembled, from fear or excitement—it didn't matter. She was her king's subject, to do with as he pleased. And right now it pleased him to fuck her. Right here, in the chamber he created to demonstrate the wealth and power he had accumulated throughout the years. His bed was finely carved *tavis* wood and a natural spring served as his bath. There was a round banquet table and four chairs off to the right. Yes. He was proud of this chamber, proud of the craftsmanship and proud of the conquering that brought him such wealth.

Let the wench taste it, if only for a night.

With one hand, he cupped the nape of the woman's neck and pulled her to him. Then he crushed his lips against hers in a punishing kiss. She melted against him. No fight. No struggle. She only choked once as he pushed his tongue deep into her mouth.

Yes, yes. Complete submission. Her training was going well.

The moment she seemed to be enjoying his touch, he broke the kiss and let her see the rage in his eyes. "I'm going to fuck you now. I'm going to pound you hard, until you can't breathe. Until you can't walk."

The woman's gasp made his blood boil all the hotter.

"As you wish, Sire," she whispered, trembling, and bowed her head.

"Get on the table and spread your legs."

Without hesitation she did his bidding. Her lissome figure slid upon the cool wood, and gooseflesh rose across her soft skin. Her nipples tightened, drawing into taut beads. On her back, she parted her thighs, her ass resting just at the edge of the wood.

"Wider," he growled. He could smell her womanly juices as she opened herself to him, presenting her pink, swollen flesh. He approached, knowing he had to taste her before he fucked her.

With a swift shrug of his shoulders, he sent his robe slithering from his muscular body. His long black hair brushed the skin of his shoulders. For a moment he wondered if his dark eyes burned with the same fire racing through his veins.

Should I torture her first? A whip or tool in his hands would not be wise at this moment, when such fury filled him. *But there are other things I can do.*

He grinned.

Balin cupped her breast, then with great force he twisted her nipple. She screamed, her body writhing. Her head tilted back as she cried out, exposing her pale throat.

There was something musical in a woman's cry of pain and pleasure that sent his lust raging. With a twirl of his fingers, he forced another shriek from her trembling lips.

Positioning himself between her thighs, his cock nudged her moist folds. He raked his fingernails from her shoulders to her breasts, scraping each sensitive nipple. He continued down to her stomach, leaving eight angry red lines.

Her breaths were small pants and she whimpered. He knew his marks burned. He blew lightly on them to increase the sensation.

As he made to taste the woman, a knock sounded on his door. His hands had settled on the woman's hips. They tightened, fingers digging into soft flesh.

Another knock.

"What?"

"I have news of the *bakirs*." Olin's muffled response made Balin's jaw snap shut. So much for the tasting. It was time to clear his senses.

"Enter." As Balin spoke, he stood straight and thrust his cock into the woman's waiting pussy. Her back arched on impact, her breath catching. Her cove was small, tight. But as he forced himself further, pumped in and out, her body yielded and let him drive deeper.

Olin opened the door and stepped inside, immediately dropping to one knee. He bowed his head. "Lord Kir has the woman."

Balin's pulse jumped, his hips slamming into the woman's pussy hard. She groaned, squirming against him.

"Do you know what it cost me to have that woman brought here? The magic that I spent?" Balin's tone dropped, menace in his rasping voice.

"Yes, M'Lord." Olin remained in the subservient position, eyes downcast.

"Where is my captain?" Balin's hips thrust forward again and again. The sound of flesh slapping flesh filled the room.

Olin's body trembled. "The werewolves captured him along with the others. Only one *bakir* escaped."

In a rage, Balin pushed from the table, jerking out of the woman's body. His cock arched angrily, its head full and purple, bursting with blood beneath the thin skin. He spun to face Olin. "Kill the surviving traitor. I will take care of those imprisoned by Kir."

Balin swept up his robe from the floor, his arms pushing through the long sleeves. As he drew the sash around him, he paused. His gaze went back to the woman sprawled upon the table, legs still parted.

"Leave me, Bella." His harsh command made the woman hasten off the table and out of the room, leaving her clothes where they lay.

"On second thought, bring the traitor to me. I will teach him to never leave his unit."

Olin flinched and rose to his feet.

Slowly he backed out of the room, leaving Balin alone in his fury.

Chapter Five

ဢ

In the war room, Lord Kir studied the perfectly scaled model that encompassed his own realm, as well as the Kingdoms of Tarok and the Kingdom of Malachad.

"Here," his First Captain Janan said, pointing a thick finger to the land that separated the mountains of Malachad and Oz. Not far from the place where he had found Abby. "Our scouts spotted several *bakirs*. Apparently they were scouting our realm for signs of weakness."

Kir growled. "And what happened to these *bakirs*?"

Janan clenched his fist on the table beside the model, his blue eyes flashing with anger. "We captured all but one. The *bakir* escaped, surely returning to his master." A frustrated breath brushed a strand of his dusky hair from his eyes.

"Then you have prisoners." Kir dismissed the *bakir* who had escaped. "We shall interrogate them with whatever means necessary." He gave Janan a nod. "See to it they reveal what Balin is up to — no matter what it takes."

Janan bowed and shifted into a sable-haired wolf even as he turned and bounded away.

"M'Lord," came Lan's voice behind him.

Kir turned, hands behind his back and stance wide as he waited for his warrior to speak.

"The wench. The one you call Abby." Lan cleared his throat. "She managed to free herself and escape with that beast of hers."

For a moment Kir was too stunned to speak. *No one* had *ever* dared to throw off a punishment he had assigned. To walk away from his orders. An enemy would not have lived. A member of his clan wouldn't dare to try.

"Shall we send a search team to find her?" Lan asked.

Kir hardened his features. "I will take care of the wench myself."

Fire burned his veins as he shifted and at the same time tore into a dead run. He was so furious that it emanated off him in waves. His people stayed well out of his way while he plowed through the cavern.

Who did the wench think she was, defying him? His people knew he would never tolerate such outright impudence, that anyone who challenged him would be justly punished.

At his simple mind command the great golden doors leading out of Emerald City opened. Kir's keen sense of smell caught Abby's vanilla scent and the smell of O as they fled along the Yellow Road. Obviously moving toward the red beast she had ridden to Oz.

Her scent became stronger as he loped down the tree-shaded path. Early morning sun dappled through the leaves onto the road and the wind smelled of a coming storm.

As he came out of the trees he saw a very naked Abby opening the door of the red machine and ushering O into its depths.

Her scent—gods. The lusciousness of her finely sculpted figure made his body ache, made the primal beast within him want to roar.

Instead he paused to howl. A long, commanding howl that shattered the air with his dominance. Staking his territory, which included the beautiful woman before him.

Abby's gaze shot to him and terror washed her features. "A wolf. Shit."

She scrambled into the car and slammed the door shut just as Kir arrived.

He rested on his haunches for a moment, his gaze narrowed on the woman who had dared to defy him.

"Oh, my god, Otto," he heard her say through the sandglass that was cracked like a giant spider web. She fumbled with something in the car, her gaze tearing from it to Kir and back. "It's a freaking *wolf*."

The red machine suddenly made a strange noise and Kir resisted stepping back. A sound like *ch-ch-ch-ch* came from it at the same time Abby was saying, "Ohshitohshitohshit."

Enough, Kir thought and slowly began to shift.

Abby's gaze shot to him again. Her jaw dropped. The machine's noise faltered. It stopped completely as her gaze rose up to meet his eyes when he was fully transformed.

"Kir—the wolf—you. Oh, shit." She fumbled again and he heard a clicking noise. A whirring sound, and then a loud roar as the red beast vibrated, came to life. A puff of gray smoke shot out from beneath the contraption, and the stench was nearly overpowering. This time it took everything he had not to show his surprise at the growling noise the machine made. Instead of backing up he took a step closer and glared at her through the crackled sandglass.

"Get out now," he commanded.

"Fuck you." Eyes still on him, Abby shifted a black knob. The machine's strange wheels spun in the grass and the vehicle tore backward, away from him. Grass, dirt and rocks flew into the air from the strange wheels as the car spun in a U-shaped turn.

Abby moved her hand again and the red beast shot forward and tore down the Yellow Road.

Kir had never seen anything like it. No mode of transportation in Oz or Tarok moved so quickly. He shifted into wolf form and bolted after the red beast. A werewolf could move unnaturally fast, but it was almost difficult to keep up with the vehicle. Through the back sandglass he saw Abby cast glances over her shoulder. The beast roared again and shot forward.

Just as Kir thought she was going to outrun him, the contraption coughed. Sputtered. Slowed down.

Abby's cry of "No, no, no!" came from the machine. It jerked forward then sputtered again and slowly rolled to a stop.

When Kir loped up to the door, Abby was banging her forehead against the round wheel that she gripped tight in her hands. "Goddamn gas tank. Forgot to fill the tank. Oh, shit. What am I going to do now? Damn. Damn. Damn," she added, punctuating each word by banging her head against the wheel.

Kir shifted into his naked man's form. Folded his arms and watched her. She refused to look at him. O put his paws on the sandglass from his place behind Abby and wagged his tail. He barked, showing his pleasure at seeing Kir.

Kir smirked.

"Traitor," Abby muttered, her forehead still against the wheel.

Kir widened his stance and tossed his head back. "Get out."

Abby stilled. "Fuck you," she said again without looking at him.

"That will come later," he said, his cock stirring at the thought. "But first you must be punished for your defiance."

Abby slowly raised her head, her cinnamon eyes flashing dark fire that only raised the temperature of his blood. It surprised him how much her fiery nature pleased him.

"This is the United States, you big dumbass." Her glare never wavered. "I'm a free woman. I don't answer to you or anyone else."

Kir paused as something stirred in his memory. "Is San Francisco in this United States?"

She folded her arms across her chest, covering her luscious breasts. "As if you don't know that already."

He chuckled, unable to hide a smile. "Then you come from the same world as the Tarok Queens." Kir shook his head. "It is not a wonder, then, why you do not know our ways. The Queens required much training, as you will."

He chuckled again thinking of the irony of the fates— how they had delivered the Tarok Kings their mates and how the winds had delivered...his?

His mirth faded quickly.

He didn't know this woman. He certainly couldn't be thinking of her as more than his possession. If he did, he might turn into a besotted fool, just as his kingly friends became once they snared their women.

Abby clenched her fists on the wheel in front of her, so tight her knuckles went bone-white. "I've had enough of this," she said through clenched teeth. "Go away. I'll find my own way home from this freaked-out place."

This time it was anger that flooded Kir's veins. All mirth, all patience, fled him. "You will get out of that machine, or I will take you out."

She raised her hand, extending only her middle finger in a gesture that was no doubt intended to be offensive. "Bite me," she said.

"If you insist." He walked around the front of the vehicle, studying the fractured sandglass. He continued to the side where there was an empty seat and the sandglass was unbroken.

"I hope you brought a very big can opener, wolf-man, because I'm not coming out and you're not getting in."

Lacing his fingers, he clenched them tight together. With all his might, he brought his fists down on the sandglass.

It shattered.

Abby screamed. O barked.

The glass still clung together, as if the pieces were held with some kind of adhesive. Kir studied it for a moment. Abby looked shaken. She swallowed, her gaze darting from the bowed, broken glass to his face.

He'd been careful to hit the glass so that shards would scatter away from Abby and O. Now all it would take was one more hit and he'd be able to crawl through the glass and force her out of the machine.

He raised his fists again.

"All right!" Abby shouted. "Allrightallrightallright." She went to open the door and rolled her eyes. "I didn't even have the damn door locked."

Slowly she climbed from the vehicle, O bounding out after her.

She glanced at the dog. "You're an Irish wolfhound. He's a wolf-man. You can take him on, right?"

The dog trotted up to Kir and rubbed his nose under Kir's palm, obviously asking to be petted.

"Still a traitor," she grumbled.

He rubbed the animal's head and scratched behind its ears as he studied Abby. She had her arms folded across her breasts, the morning sun teasing fiery red glints from her hair.

She was magnificent. Wild.

And it would be his pleasure to tame her.

When he walked around to where Abby stood on the Yellow Road, she raised her chin. He pushed the red beast's door shut and it gave a solid metal thunk. O trotted up to sit between the two of them, looking hopefully from one to the other.

"Just think *neuter*," Abby said in a low growl.

O whined. Kir winced, then sighed.

He was weary of her defiance. Instead of putting up with any more of her rude comments and resistance, he simply grabbed her by the waist and flung her over his shoulder.

Abby screamed in fury. She struggled and fought like a weretiger, clawing at his back and trying her best to kick him.

By the gods. Perhaps she's related to Tarok's people after all. I should ask. If she doesn't dig out my heart before I get her back to Oz.

Kir clasped her tight around her thighs, pinning them together so that she couldn't move her legs. Then with his open palm he swatted her hard against both ass cheeks.

Abby cried out and stopped clawing him. He spanked her again, hard.

"Damn you," she said, but he smelled the scent of her desire, felt the tightness of her nipples against his back.

She wasn't entirely unwilling, no matter what she would like him to think.

He started walking down the Yellow Road, back to Emerald City. After a few seconds he flattened his hand against her ass once again.

"Ow, bastard!" she cried, but he felt tremors running through her as if she were close to orgasm.

"Do not climax without my permission, wench," he said as he continued to walk with her slung over his shoulder. "And you must always refer to me as M'Lord."

"When Hell—" she started to say, then he settled his palm on her ass. "Uh, yeah. I mean *yes, M'Lord.*"

Kir almost laughed at her spirit and knew he was in for a most enjoyable time indeed. He would make certain there would be no freeing herself from her bonds, no escaping.

He slipped his fingers between Abby's slick thighs. The corner of his mouth curved as he felt her wetness, her obvious arousal. She gasped, and he could tell she was holding back a moan of desire.

"Stop it already," she said, her voice coming out breathy and edgy.

"I think not." He enjoyed the feel of her slick folds beneath his fingers, the way her thighs trembled when he rubbed her tight nub with his thumb, and the way she cried out when he thrust two fingers into her quim.

Her scent—an aphrodisiac to his senses. Her juices flowed over his fingers and he brought them to his mouth and sucked. Ah, gods, her taste was definitely a fine nectar he would enjoy again and again. He slipped his fingers back into her quim and pumped them in and out like he wanted to be thrusting his cock within her right this minute.

But no. This woman had not earned an orgasm or his cock. She had earned far too many punishments.

Just as he felt her near the peak of climax, he slipped his fingers out of her quim, laid his palm on her ass and squeezed the soft flesh. He thought she said, "You bastard," between clenched teeth, but her voice was too low for him to hear her clearly.

When he reached the gates to Emerald City, Kir used his magic to open the magnificent gold doorways. He strode into his city of glittering, glowing emeralds.

Abby sucked in her breath and he knew she couldn't help but admire what she could see from her upside down position. O trotted at his side, his gaze darting from werewolf to those in human form. Kir could tell O trusted him and Abby but no one else in the realm.

Smart beast.

As he strode through the great hall, Abby's fine ass received appreciative glances from males in his pack and many of the females as well.

At first he felt a sense of pride that his treasure was so admired, but then his gut clenched at the thought of any other man even close to her. The feeling was completely irrational.

"Please let me down," Abby said a little more contritely, but he had the feeling she would go for his bollocks if he did not have her properly restrained.

"Address me properly, wench." Kir slapped her ass and she yelped.

"Please, M'Lord," she said, obviously having to force out the words.

"When I am prepared to release you, I will." Kir swatted her ass again and she whimpered. The bright shade of pink on her cheeks pleased him and he looked forward to having her on her hands and knees, fucking her from behind.

At the mere thought, Kir's cock hardened painfully and he gritted his teeth.

Taking it slow with this wench would be no easy matter.

By the time he reached the dungeon, Abby had relaxed. Some. He still felt and sensed her fury at her capture.

Kir stopped in front of the dungeon doors and cut his gaze to O. "Stay," he commanded.

O sat on his haunches and whined.

Abby placed her hands on Kir's ass and lifted herself. "Don't lock him out—er, M'Lord. Please."

Without responding, Kir strode through the wooden doors and used his magic to slam them behind him. With a flick of his finger, the bars slid through their housings to lock the doors.

He slowly slid Abby down his length and nearly groaned at the feel of her soft skin gliding over his. When she stood before him on the stone floor, her hands were on his shoulders, her nipples hard buds against his chest. Her lips were parted and her cinnamon eyes darkened with passion. No matter her anger, she still wanted him.

As much as he wanted her.

He lowered his mouth, claimed hers in a hard, dominating kiss. She was his. By all the gods, she belonged to him.

So very sweet. So very lovely.

So full of fire.

He grasped her small ass in his hands, yanking her body tight against his as he thrust his tongue into her mouth. Abby didn't fight him. She took him willingly and gave back just as much. She linked her fingers around his neck and pressed her naked body closer to his, so close he could feel her nest of curls against his leg. He pressed his leg between hers and she rode it, rubbing her wet folds along his thigh.

Soft sighs escaped her as he tangled his tongue with hers, then bit her lower lip. To his surprise she bit him back, and he growled at the feel of her small teeth sinking into his lower lip. A sharp pain that eased into pleasure, that made him demand more of her.

When he finally pulled away from the kiss and raised his head, Abby just stared up at him with a dazed look in her beautiful eyes. "You're the enemy," she said with a shiver in her voice. "Why the hell am I enjoying kissing you so much? You've kidnapped me, stolen my clothes, tied me up, made my Irish wolfhound go traitor on me, and you're some kind of wolf-man, er, werewolf."

"M'Lord," he reminded her as sternly as he could manage. "Your punishments continue to mount. Perhaps, though, I will reduce the number in consideration of the fact that you are a stranger to my land and our laws."

Abby released her hold on his neck and tried to push away but he still gripped her buttocks tightly. "That's generous of you, er, M'Lord."

"I know."

Abby rolled her eyes but quickly lowered her gaze when he gave her a fierce look. He released her ass, took her by the hand and led her toward the X-shaped cross that stood upon a platform in one corner of the dungeon.

"Uh, what are you doing with me?" she asked, and hurried to add, "M'Lord."

"Quiet, wench." He led her up the three steps of the wooden platform until they were in front of the X-cross. He felt her tremble as he took her by the shoulders and pushed her back up against the padded wood.

"You're not going to do what I think you are…" Her voice trailed off as her eyes widened.

"M'Lord," he reminded her yet again. This wench was really beginning to try his patience.

She visibly swallowed as he grabbed one of her wrists. In a lightning-fast movement he cuffed the wrist in velvet-lined metal. He produced a key with his magic and locked the cuff.

"Uh-uh, no way." Abby aimed her knee with a quick movement to his groin and he barely dodged it.

She tried to fight him, kick him, bite him, as he locked her other wrist to the cross, then each of her ankles.

By the time he finished, she was breathing hard, her hair a wild mass of auburn curls around her face, sweaty tendrils clinging to her forehead. He stepped back to admire her lovely body displayed for his view. Her breasts were forced out, perfect for him to suck. Her folds were exposed to him and her scent was rich with desire. He looked forward to running his tongue along the faerie kisses sprinkled across her shoulders and her chest. All that soft, lovely, pale skin would soon be pink from his flogger.

And he would make sure she enjoyed every minute of it.

But her eyes—her glare would have melted a glacier. "Bastard," she spit out.

Ignoring her, he walked over to a wall lined with crops, whips and other tools. He chose a black leather flogger with soft leather straps that would give a fine sting to her fair skin.

When he pivoted so that he was facing her again, he ran the leather straps over his hand and studied her features. Her glare hadn't wavered, despite the fact she knew she was about to be punished.

"Oh, wait," she said with a sarcastic edge to her voice. "That should have been M'Lord Bastard."

Chapter Six

&

When will you ever learn to keep your mouth shut? Abby asked herself.

Much to her surprise the whipping didn't start immediately. Instead, Lord Kir ran the handle of the flogger up her arm. The roughened leather caused goose bumps to pebble her skin as he moved over her shoulder, across her neck, and then slid between her small breasts. Her nipples shamefully hardened. Tiny knobs swelled on her darkened areolas.

He smiled.

Well, damn it. All she needed was for this man to think she wanted him to flog her.

The handle grazed her ribcage, caressed her stomach and stopped to tangle in her nest of hair below. The tingle in her breasts became an aching need. Not to mention the dull, pulsating sensation that began between her thighs. Abby forced herself to inhale, holding back the tremor that made her jaws lock tight when he brushed the handle along her inner thighs and then against her slit.

She was helpless, defenseless, as her juices flowed over the lightly probing whip. Her pussy pulsed with each stroke, building her need for fulfillment. The knowledge that a man controlled her body was frustrating. But damn it, what could she do bound, spread-eagle—wide open for the man's pleasure as he tormented her? And torment her he did, by rubbing that damn thing across her slit, pushing her to the brink of release. Then just before she reached out to touch heaven, he stopped—pulled away—leaving her aching for relief.

Her scent was heavy on the whip as he brought the leather to her lips. "Kiss my shaft," he demanded.

"Kiss my ass," she retorted and raised her chin. Two could play this game.

He licked his lips like her suggestion was something to think about.

Man, she had shit for brains. Here she was cuffed to a cross and she continued to antagonize her kidnapper. Not to mention she was already perched on the edge of a climax, with wolf-man holding the reins and ready to snatch it away at any time.

Lord Kir firmly pressed the handle to her mouth. "You will learn to obey me in all things," he said softly. His air of authority was hard to miss. This was a man used to getting what he wanted. "Submit to me, Abby. It is your path to happiness." He applied more pressure to the whip. "Now, kiss the shaft."

Abby tasted herself and the leather as it squeezed beyond her lips. One thing she had never done was sample her own juices. She found it heady, if not arousing. She even found the man's dominance exciting.

I'm losing my mind.

Lord Kir moved the handle of the flogger from her mouth and took one step backward. He snapped the flogger and the straps landed gently on her thigh.

That wasn't too bad. Abby relaxed as he struck the opposite thigh, a little harder this time.

Damn him. And damn the fact that it actually felt good.

"I won't ever surrender, so you might as well give up and let me go home," she said even though she was getting totally turned on.

With the palm of his hand Lord Kir rubbed her thigh and then the other. Her flesh came alive beneath his touch, tingling and burning.

Yes, yes. Stroke higher, higher. Abby held her breath, willing him to touch her, caress her pussy.

This time when the whip snapped and made contact, the pain to her thigh stung like a son of a bitch. She flinched, forcing back a scream that knotted in her throat. But what pissed her off was how it actually made her hornier. Crap. How could a whipping make her even *more* aroused?

No way would she give this man, wolf—whatever the hell he was—the satisfaction of knowing that last blow had hurt and that she had ended up enjoying it. She tried to relax, knowing that if she tensed the discomfort would deepen.

The next flogger strike landed hard on her other thigh, making pink stripes, one for each of the thongs that bit into her flesh. Again, he teased her with the soft straps, caressing her with them, waking her skin so it was more sensitive to the flogging.

The next lash caused her to suck in her lower lip. Tears welled in her eyes despite the fact that her core had grown wetter. Her nipples ached to be sucked and she was almost ready to do anything he asked if only he'd fuck her.

Well, almost—but not quite. Abby still had a little fight in her.

Then Lord Kir did the oddest thing. He knelt before her, and in long, wet strokes he licked her abused skin, cooling the burn, easing the pain.

His ministrations started just above her right knee, slowly moving upwards. Each caress of his tongue was soothing, sensual. The deep massage the back of her leg received from his gentle hands was more than stimulating. It was a touch that had her hungry to be lavished in other places, mainly her throbbing slit.

As if Lord Kir read her mind, he buried his nose into her moist heat. She heard his long, drawn-out inhale. He growled low in his throat before burrowing deeper.

The feel of his lips on her swollen folds was her undoing. His mouth and tongue worked together to form a vacuum that made Abby feel as if he was drinking from her pussy. When his tongue flicked over her clit, her knees buckled. Only her bound wrists held her upright.

Oh man – oh man. Her core quivered. The ache grew with each touch of his tongue.

Desperately, Abby fought the conflicting emotions that assailed her. He was her enemy, her captor. Yet her hips moved to the rhythm of his strokes. Even her nipples screamed to be pinched, teased and sucked by this man. The need to feel his hands, his mouth on her breasts was overwhelming.

As Abby's climax coiled low in her belly, she arched into him. "Finally," she gasped.

The suction broke, his tongue stilled.

Hanging on the edge of the precipice, she waited for him to take her over the pinnacle. She held her breath and waited—and waited.

Instead he moved to her other thigh and began to administer long, wet licks to her hot flesh. He took great care in ensuring every inch of tortured skin was attended to.

Abby sagged against her bonds in frustration. *Well, shit. Finish the job, wolf-man, or I'll do it myself.*

It was obvious that completing what he had started wasn't his intent. Abby clenched the muscles in her pussy and rolled her hips. Begged her body to give her what she needed. Usually, she could come in a heartbeat, especially when she was so close to the crest, but strangely it felt like this man controlled her. That she hungered for his touch to complete her. Frustrated, she bit the inside of her cheek to stop herself from screaming out loud.

She might refuse to let his actions make her cry, but her pussy grew wet under his command, then shut down on his demand. And she didn't like it, not one damn bit.

As her desire unraveled, so did her patience. "Quit drooling on me, wolf-man, and let me go."

Lord Kir's husky growl was almost inaudible, as if forced through clenched teeth. The tendons in his bare shoulders were tight ribbons of tension as he rose. When his heated glare met hers, Abby realized her off-color comment had lit a flame in his eyes hot enough to ignite a bonfire.

She'd really pissed him off this time.

A shiver of fear raced up her spine. She bit down hard on her bottom lip, resisting the urge to beg for mercy.

Even stretched to his limits the man held himself in complete control. With a flick of his wrist he brought the flogger down softly on one breast. The thongs were light streaks of lightning across her globe, causing an incredible sensation when the tips stung her nipple.

She screamed. The pain was incredible. The sting amazing—and she loved it! Abby had always wondered what bittersweet really meant. Now she knew. It was pain blended with overtones of pleasure. And she wanted more. Her body shouted for more.

Of course, breasts were nothing but fatty tissue anyway. And a woman's nipples were made to take abuse, Abby's nipples probably more than others. Because there wasn't anything she liked better than to have her nipples pinched and played with. And she wanted them played with *now*.

"Bastard," she shrieked. Hot, liquid heat raced through her veins as she urged him on. She was going to come this time with or without him. All she had to do was force his hand.

When the leather touched only her nipple, she groaned low. Her eyelashes fluttered as she savored the intense feelings that filtered through her. *Ahhh.* A tremor shook her. The delicious wave swept from her head to her toes, drawing her closer to that elusive orgasm.

Another, she cried silently. But when nothing happened she knew Lord Kir needed a little more encouragement.

"Prick." The insult came out on a breathless sigh.

Still Abby didn't feel the sting she craved. She waited a heartbeat. Then one eyelid crept up followed by the other. What faced her should have scared the shit out of her but all she could do was burst into laughter.

The man was furious.

His eyes glazed with anger. The heaving of his broad chest made him look as if he was about to explode. Clearly, he didn't know what to do with her and it frustrated the hell out of him.

Her laughter died when Lord Kir's body began to twitch. She heard bones crack. Muscles popped, and her jaw dropped at each crunch and distorted movement his body made. Then hair sprung from the man's pores as his gorgeous body morphed, shape-shifting into a beautiful and very large golden wolf. The animal's sapphire glare pinned her, as if it alone held her bound to the cross.

Abby pulled in a tight breath as reality hit. She wasn't in Kansas or even in Tennessee. In fact, she wasn't on planet Earth anymore. Somehow the tornado had thrown her into another dimension, another place where magic existed and people turned into wolves. Where domination, submission and erotic torture were acceptable. And one man, this man, believed that he owned her.

Suddenly all her confidence, all her cockiness vanished. She was by herself in this whacked-out world. O was even being held from her.

Oh, god, I am truly alone.

The bar across the door miraculously rose from its hinges. The door flung open crashing against the wall. O barked, wagged his tail and attempted to go to Abby, but Lord Kir in wolf-form yipped, driving the dog backwards to follow him out of the room.

The doors slammed shut.

Oh, yes. She was well and truly alone.

Chapter Seven

ଛେ

The silence was deafening.

The illuminated green walls began to dim until Abby was thrown into pitch darkness. The air seemed to thicken and it suddenly felt harder to breathe.

She hiccupped. How in the world had she gotten into this mess? Was this even real, or had she totally lost her mind? She was beginning to think the latter.

Her thoughts turned to her family, and an ache gripped her heart as she found herself missing Uncle Henry, O, and the parents she'd never known. She even missed Aunt Maye. God, she hoped Aunt Maye had survived the tornado. The woman was on the harsh side, but Abby truly loved her aunt.

A masculine voice startled her and she snapped her head up.

I would never leave you alone like the Lord of the mountain dwelling cave wolves. The deep tone was beautiful and soothing, almost lyrical.

"Who—who are you?" Abby hiccupped again, wishing it wasn't dark so that she could see whoever was talking.

I am your friend, Abby. Possibly your only friend in this strange world you have been thrown into. And I am close. Not within this room, but close. His voice so soft and alluring it wrapped around her, giving her a sense of security—but not quite. She hesitated, trying to think clearly, but for some reason her thoughts seemed fuzzy. Off.

"I don't have any friends here." Abby held on to that belief even though a part of herself realized she had enjoyed Kir's dominance.

Except that he had left her. Alone.

Yet now she didn't feel alone anymore. The caress of the stranger's voice brought her a level of comfort in the dark. She realized he wasn't in the room with her but in her mind. She felt him there, and somehow it felt natural.

I will come to you, he said.

In her mind's eye a gray shape emerged. The outline of a man. Then a dark vision of a warrior appeared. It was in the fearless cut of his jaw, the pride in the slight lift of his chin, his dignified stance. Flowing black hair brushed broad shoulders. His sharp intelligent blue eyes pinned her, raising the hair on her arms. His biceps were huge. The air of danger that surrounded him like a weapon only made him more attractive, as did the hieroglyphics tattooed on each cheekbone, the sign of infinity, a figure eight lying sideways, with a bold line above the symbol. In fact, if Abby hadn't known better she would have sworn he had been ripped from the pages of some book on the gladiator days.

He reached out to her. Mesmerized, she stared at his large hand. The gold ring on his index finger carried the same symbol as those tattooed on his face, and it glowed as if a raging fire had been trapped inside.

The man bowed. When he rose she thought she heard him whisper, *Take my hand. Come to me.*

Instead his voice broke into her reverie.

I can take you home, my pretty. Has Lord Kir offered you freedom and safe passage?

Silence was her answer.

I thought not. The man's tone embraced her with its warmth. Then he smiled. A ray of hope filtered through

Abby, as if his presence radiated power, power he was sharing through her vision.

"Are you a wizard?" *Duh*, that was stupid. This wasn't the Wizard of Oz. Yes, her given name might be Dorothy, but she was stark naked, strapped to a cross, minus the oh-so-important ruby-red slippers and magic words that had taken the real Dorothy home.

The man's laughter was gentle, soothing her fears.

Colors and shapes began to form around him until he was standing in a field of knee-high grass. A gentle breeze caressed the green blades, making them sway to the tune of a lullaby playing softly in her head. In the distance was a verdant forest. A lazy stream curved along its border, then disappeared around a bend. The scene was blissful, placing her slightly off-guard. She sighed.

My pretty, you do not need red shoes and nonsense words. You need a friend — a man who cares, who knows how you got here, and who knows where to find the door between the realms. I am such a man. I can fulfill your dreams and desires.

More hope rose within Abby. The knot of tension began to unwind. She'd give anything to believe the dark stranger. "Who are you?"

He hesitated before he said, *I am Balin, ruler of the Kingdom of Malachad.*

The image of the field of grass shifted, replaced by a majestic castle surrounded by imposing mountains. Balin stood in a wooded area, a part of his realm. He was proud and formidable, a king. The picture made Abby catch her breath.

If I were not a friend, would I share with you a name that enrages Lord Kir and all his clan? Again he reached out to her. Again she heard his hypnotic voice whisper, *Take my hand. Come to me.*

Abby was so confused. She didn't know what was real and what wasn't any more. Through the haze she struggled to think. "Then you aren't Lord Kir's friend? Not one of his allies?"

His laughter filled her head with warmth and reassurance. *I think not, my pretty.* The smile he flashed her almost made Abby's toes curl. God, he was gorgeous.

So is Kir, said a tiny voice deep in her mind. *There's more to that wolf-man than you'd like to admit.*

His blue eyes…

The way he looked at her…

His tender caress…

His kisses…

His genuine frustration at not being able to make her cower and heel…

Yet the light in his eyes each time they butted heads. He relished the fight as much as she did.

Yes.

There was something about the damned annoying wolf-man.

I have lost my mind. No way! I'm not letting Lord *Kir seduce me. Arrogant bastard.*

"You're saying you'll help me escape?" Her bound body shivered with hope and sorrow, as if she didn't really want to leave. Now where the hell did the sorrow come from?

Yes. Balin's voice was deep and reassuring.

Escape. Yes. That's what she wanted, right? Of course. She didn't belong here. Kir was a possessive jerk. These wolf-people were alien, too different…

Or am I the different one?

Either way she was tired, confused, and so very lonely.

Abby blinked and the scene within her head changed yet again. A gentle snow fell on an already white haven, Balin's castle, his kingdom. Delicate flakes floated gently before her eyes.

Now sleep, my pretty. Sleep. When you wake, you must convince Lord Kir that you are willing to do his bidding. She felt the thrust of his words lulling her to sleep. *Should you fail you will not be allowed freedom, freedom which will lead you to me — to where you belong.*

Abby's eyes grew heavy. She tried to fight the voice's strong push to obey, but she yawned and her eyes watered. "How will I get in contact with you?" she asked, her words coming out almost slurred.

Not to worry. I will find you. Now sleep. Sleep…

Chapter Eight

ဘ

"Please don't leave me," Abby whimpered as Balin's voice grew faint. Her tone sounded desperate and youthful to her own ears as she felt the tug of slumber pull her deeper and she sagged against her bonds.

She snuggled into a light caress across her cheek. "Please don't leave me," she murmured.

"I would never leave you." The whiskey-deep voice of Kir jerked her fully awake again. This was not the man who offered to help her after Kir had left her alone for who knows how long.

This was the bastard. Her enemy.

A single tear of disappointment rolled down her cheek.

Lord Kir's tongue slid across her face wiping away the tear. "My little kitten, don't cry. It is difficult to accept a new world, a new Master."

Abby startled at the light pressure against her mouth when his lips met hers.

"Do not continue to fight me." He kissed her again. "If you give yourself to me, if you submit, it will make the adjustment easier." He continued to stroke her face with his fingers. She heard a *click-click-click-click* and then the bindings encircling her wrists and ankles were released as if by magic. "I want only to see you happy."

Abby would have fallen if Lord Kir hadn't been there to catch her. Her muscles and joints ached, she needed to relieve herself, and she was thirsty and hungry. She felt like she'd been on the cross forever, but she knew it had to be only an hour, tops.

Gently Kir cradled her in his arms, pressing her firmly to his naked chest. "Will you submit to me, kitten?"

Balin's words came to her and she realized she needed to convince Lord Kir she would do his biddings.

Damn.

But if she was ever going to get out of Lord Kir's realm…

Sucking in her breath, forcing her muscles to obey, she nodded.

The man must have had animal sight because even in the pitch black of the room she was certain he saw her response.

"Then let us begin anew. Answer me out loud and address me properly."

"Yes," she sniffled, "M'Lord."

"I am pleased," he said.

His chest pressed into her naked flesh as he shifted her in his arms and began walking. Abby's spirits started to rise. Just knowing that she wasn't alone and that Balin would be there to help her escape gave her new courage.

Yet she could barely think at that moment. The way Kir's flesh rubbed against hers made her want him with a wild and crazy yearning. The untamed, earthy smell of his skin made her long to taste him.

Now if she only had a brain—or used what she had wisely—she could maneuver herself to more freedom, to that precious chance for escape.

What would a submissive say now? Oh, yeah.

"It pleases me to please you, M'Lord."

The man drew to an abrupt halt, jarring her. Tension rippled across his body like dark undercurrents in a dangerous river.

"Do not seek to placate me, wench." The tenderness in his voice had vanished. His once gentle hands became firm. Fire sparked off the wall with his anger and filled the room with a green glow as emeralds captured the flames.

Shit. She'd overplayed that one. Well? It wasn't like she had a clue how to be submissive. Submissive just wasn't in her blood.

When it grew light enough for Abby to see Kir's face, his expression was hard, his glare intense.

She should hate this man, but her heartbeat quickened. Her nipples hardened and ached. Damn the man and whatever magic he used to bewitch her.

Or was it the bad boy gravitational pull? That *thing* that always got her in trouble? That dangerous, almost forbidden mien that said, "If you touch you'll get burned". It drove her wild. She wanted a taste of forbidden fruit, wanted what she couldn't or shouldn't have.

But he was her enemy.

Still Abby couldn't help feeling the need to run her fingers through his golden mane, hair that glistened like precious gems in the rays of light beaming off the walls. She had an almost uncontrollable urge to cup his face, erase the lines of stress furrowing his brow, and kiss him as he held her cradled in his arms.

No.

No, no, no.

This man was holding her hostage. Keeping her against her will. A constrictor knot on the testicles would be too good for him. Maybe Balin would help her do that.

But…

Damn it.

Lord Kir confused her senses. Tender one moment and demanding the next. He inflamed her sensuality like no other man had. Her mind told her no but her body yelled, "Hell yeah!"

Is it magic? Or was it the fact that the man was a gorgeous specimen of male, whether man or beast?

And there was something else about him beneath his arrogant demeanor, something that told her he was more than what he appeared to be. Beneath it all she sensed that this man was deep, sensitive.

"I-I just don't like the cross, M'Lord. I'll do anything not to be tied to that thing again." Abby held a tight breath under Lord Kir's scrutiny. When his hands softened around her body and he took a step forward and then another, she exhaled.

Yes.

At the end of the long corridor they were met by Linara, the woman Abby had seen fucked simultaneously by two men. Just the sight of her, the memory of that unbelievably hot threesome, dampened the area between Abby's thighs. She swore Kir's embrace grew warmer. What would it be like to have traded places with the woman, to be fucked by two men at once, while another flogged and watched? The dark-haired woman had enjoyed it.

Would Abby?

Oh yeah, now *this* mental image had the makings of a wet dream.

Oblivious to the lightning storm happening under Abby's skin, the woman stood in a submissive position, her head bowed, hands behind her back and her feet a shoulders-width apart.

"M'Lord." Linara's voice was soft and alluring. Through dark, feathered eyelashes she glanced at Lord Kir. Her expression was sultry. The heated look of lust was obvious.

Reflexively, Abby ground her teeth. Okay, so the woman was beautiful with her flowing black hair and her fashion model face. Yes, Linara's breasts were twice, no, make that three times, larger then hers. But, damn it, did the woman have to look at Kir that way? Why couldn't the trip down the corridor have taken hours, giving her more time with Kir?

Why do I care anyway? Let her look. Let her ride him hard and put him up wet, so long as he doesn't chain me to anything else.

But her teeth stayed clenched. She had to work not to clench her fists, too.

"Linara will see to your needs." Lord Kir eased Abby out of his arms onto her feet. Firm fingers pinched Abby's chin, drawing her face up so that she stared into blue eyes full of warning. "You cannot escape me, my kitten."

It was all Abby could do to keep the daggers out of her return stare.

Kir crushed his lips to hers even as he picked her up again and carried her forward. Where they were going, at that moment she didn't give a damn. When the kiss broke Abby was breathless.

He released her, slowly setting her on her feet once more. As Abby's eyes opened she found that he had carried her into another cavern, but this one looked like a bedroom with wall-to-wall white carpeting. The bed was a huge hulled-out boulder filled with pillows, blankets and furs so soft in appearance that Abby couldn't resist walking over to the bed and running her fingers through the downy fleece.

Abby had thought that since they were underground the air would feel heavy, smell musty. But just the opposite was true. She lifted her head and inhaled. It was fresh, a clean smell, like the moment after a rain shower.

As she moved around the room, Kir's intense gaze followed her.

From behind a solid wall of rock she heard water falling. She furrowed her brows as she wondered what was on the other side.

"It is a shower," responded Linara as if she'd heard Abby's thoughts. Her soft hand grasped Abby's and she began to lead Abby straight into the rock formation.

Abby dug her heels into the soft carpet. "Wait a minute!"

The woman glanced over her shoulder and smiled. "It is an illusion, M'lady. The entrance exists."

Still Abby stood her ground. She jerked her hand trying to free herself.

"You will do as Linara requests." The warning in Lord Kir's tone put Abby's feet into motion.

And sure enough, as they approached the wall, the mystical colors of the emerald rock shifted until a large opening appeared.

This was some freaky shit. But when she turned to look at the waterfall, its exquisite beauty took her breath away. Crystal-clear turquoise water flowed from a crevasse in the rock, pooling on a floor that shimmered like glass. A small whirlpool swirled, drinking down the water, so that it didn't flood the room. Night flowers bloomed, strange-looking orchids of red, yellow and white. Vines trailed along the walls.

A gentle tug on her hand and Linara led her to another alcove. "M'lady, you may relieve yourself in here. Then I will bathe you."

Before Abby could refuse, Linara pushed her into the room that didn't have a door. Abby rounded the corner and frowned at the granite bowl in front of her. Well, it sort of looked like a toilet. Fresh water continued to gurgle and flow within the bowl, down through a black hole. The water tumbling in the bowl was like a small waterfall. She sighed.

This place was going to take some getting used to—that was, if she hung around very long.

After Abby finished, she exited, coming face to face with Linara. The woman bowed. "Your shower awaits."

Abby pulled back her hand as the woman reached for her. "I can do it myself."

No sooner did Abby finish her sentence then a growl surfaced from around the rock wall. "You will obey Linara," grumbled Kir.

Damn. Was the man going to spend the entire time guarding her? She'd hoped to be able to speak freely with Linara. Maybe elicit the woman's assistance just in case Balin was only a figment of her imagination.

Abby slipped beneath the waterfall and was surprised to find the temperature perfect—not too cold, not too warm. She had half-expected it to be ice-cold since they were beneath the earth.

When Abby tipped her head back and allowed the water to caress her, Linara flashed a wicked grin. The woman turned, retrieved a bottle and squeezed a purple gel into her hands. It smelled of wildflowers. Rubbing her palms together, Linara worked the substance into a foam. When the woman stepped toward her, Abby's eyes widened.

She wouldn't dare.

But she did.

Abby startled at the feel of Linara's soft hands on her body. Hands that roamed freely. She had never been touched like this by a woman. When Linara's palms smoothed the silky gel across Abby's breasts, the most delicious tingle tightened her nipples. Linara must have felt the same as her nubs reacted as well. Gently she kneaded Abby's naked flesh. Abby meant to withdraw, but her feet wouldn't move and her hands didn't rise to push the woman away. It was as if she had lost control of her body.

As the woman moved down Abby's abdomen, stopping to lather the curls at the apex of her thighs, Abby gasped. Fire licked her pussy. She closed her eyes, fighting the disturbing desire for the woman's hands to stroke the flames until they flashed and burned.

A troubling thought jerked her eyes open.

Kir was watching them.

His erection jutted before him. His hands curled into tight fists. The heat of desire simmered in his blue eyes. He didn't speak and Linara didn't stop her sinful massage, continuing to move down Abby's legs and up her inner thighs. Her knees buckled slightly, and she had to brace one hand against the granite wall.

The bastard was enjoying this—but Abby thought she saw something else, too. Something like jealousy, or control just before it broke into a thousand pieces.

Fine, asshole. Want to play this game? I'll show you a thing or two.

Keeping her eyes half-closed but fixed on Kir, Abby moaned and thrust her hips into Linara's caress. "Yes," she murmured. "There. Right there. Just a little more."

Linara purred, teasing her soapy curls and brushing her outer lips until Abby's moans became more real than staged.

God, she was into this. And more than into watching Kir heat to boiling. Linara slid her hand back and forth and Abby rode it, letting Kir see every delicious shiver.

He lasted about ten more seconds.

Then a growl made his thin lips tremble. "Linara, leave us." His throaty voice was deep, sultry.

Disappointment flashed in the dark-haired woman's eyes. Still, she took her oh-so-skilled hand away and bowed. "Yes, M'Lord."

As Abby watched, half-glad, half-frustrated, Linara backed away and disappeared beyond the rock wall.

When her attention turned back to Kir, Abby's heart made a mad dash to her throat. The man was on fire, and she couldn't keep her eyes off the wolf-man's cock as he approached. He was so large, hard. Just the thought of him entering her, driving between her thighs, made Abby weak.

Using the same bottle that Linara had chosen, Kir lathered his hands. Then he started massaging where Linara left off. The slow process up Abby's thighs released a wave of desire. Her breasts were heavy, aching with the need to be touched. She was hot, ready and more than willing.

As his hand touched her swollen lips, Abby's knees quivered. She might hate herself in the morning, but tonight she was going to enjoy this man. Hell, while she was trapped in this strange place she might as well enjoy all she could.

Balin told me to make him believe I'm submitting, right? So I'll submit. For now.

"You will not come without permission," Kir murmured, circling her clit in long, slow strokes

Abby couldn't think. Her head felt heavy, thick. All she could focus on was the flame licking at the walls of her pussy. "What?"

"You will not come without my permission," he repeated firmly.

"But—"

He withdrew his finger and gently pulled her into his arms. She tensed. He was doing it again, bringing her to a point where desire singed her flesh, then dousing the fire. She attempted to pull away, but his arms tightened around her.

"You must learn to trust me. Know that when the time is right you will feel pleasure like you have never experienced before."

"That's bullshit!" she growled through clenched teeth.

"You have earned a punishment," he responded in a tone that made her want to slap him.

"Fuck you — make it two." Oh shit, what had gotten into her?

"Two it is." He released her, turned, and left her standing beneath the flowing water. Her insides ached, her flesh burned. But damn it, he wasn't going to get away with treating her this way.

After Abby rinsed, she found a towel lying on a stone ledge. She dried her body and her hair the best she could, seething with each rapid pass of the towel. When she finished, she knotted the cloth in her hands and threw it to the ground, giving it a swift kick for good measure.

She entered the bedroom to find Kir sprawled upon the bed. One leg was bent, his foot lying on the bedding. She had a perfect view of his erection springing from the nest of golden hair between his thighs. All that male flesh was oh-so enticing.

If it was the last thing Abby did tonight she'd have his cock between her thighs. She'd seduce him or finish the job herself when he left her alone.

As she approached the bed he raised a hand to halt her. He pointed over her shoulder. "I have laid out your clothing for the night."

Biting back a few smart remarks Abby turned, following the path of his finger.

On a chair lay a pile of clothing that shimmered beneath the lights. When she strolled over and picked up the ensemble, she smiled. The fabric was a sheer rainbow of glistening colors. The tiny shorts and halter top would look sinful on her.

Lord Kir didn't stand a chance.

Abby turned her back to Kir. A soft growl announced his displeasure. Wiggling her ass, she moved the tight shorts up her legs and over her hips, making sure they hung low and enticing. She paused and received another rumble of impatience. She drew her hair over one shoulder, baring her back. Then she draped the halter top over her head, allowing it to brush her nipples before the fabric covered her breasts. Kir's next growl was louder, deeper. His irritability only encouraged her as she took her dear, sweet time fastening the tie into an easy-to-remove knot.

When she was dressed she pivoted to face Kir, feeling much more confident. With a sway of her hips she approached him.

Slowly.

Letting her body talk to him from beneath the unusually soft fabric.

His expression tightened and looked almost pained.

This was going well.

Abby leaned down, began to slither onto the bed—but he halted her with an upheld hand.

She rolled her eyes. *What now?*

"You have lost your right to comfort. If you want to rest in this bed, you'll earn it."

She jerked her attention in the direction he pointed. In the corner on the floor was a gigantic pillow, big enough to sleep on. No blanket, no fur, nothing else.

Anger rose within her faster and faster, like a tornado picking up speed. She whipped back around to him. Her body burned with fury. He ignored her, snuggling into his own bedding.

"Do not attempt to pleasure yourself." Kir fluffed a pillow. "The suit you wear is a chastity veil. The material numbs all feelings." He settled back on the pillow.

Well fuck! She'd show him. As she attempted to disrobe she found the material was melded to her skin. Her agitated fingers dug but never gained hold of the not-so-fascinating material.

"Shit!" she hissed.

Images of dangling Kir from the loft danced in her mind. Or she could feed him to the hogs. Hell, old Bob could probably stomp a few hoof prints into his arrogant ass...

It took all her strength to replay Balin's instructions, to remember that her compliance was her ticket out of cave-world, away from know-it-all wolf-bastards. Inwardly raging, she forced herself to walk over to the pillow. Actually, she stomped over to it.

As she plopped down she noticed a small basket.

"If you are hungry, food is in the basket for you." The son of a bitch rolled over and before she pulled a piece of bread from the woven container he was lightly snoring.

"Asshole." Abby crammed the bread into her mouth and bit down hard.

Chapter Nine

ဆ

During the night Kir found himself needing to feel the warmth of the creature who had virtually fallen into his hands. He went to the bed he had given her to lie upon and with his magic ordered the filmy restraining fabric to slip away from her body.

She was uncommonly lovely to his eyes, with a spirit that almost glowed like the cave crystals. Yet there was fear in her, and pain, and some darkness he couldn't yet identify. She was complex, his kitten.

Kir vanished her outfit back into the wardrobe. He lay down behind her, half on and half off the bed pillow. He nestled her head under his chin, draped his arm over her waist and his thigh over her hip, so that her buttocks rested against his groin. He enjoyed simply holding her, feeling her in his embrace. It was like she belonged there.

Abby murmured in her sleep but she didn't wake. He thought he heard her say *Kanzaz* and *home* and *Aunt Maye*.

His treasure did not realize it yet, but Oz was now her home. With that thought he drifted to sleep until Abby's shifting woke him again.

Even though there were no windows in the cavern Kir could instantly sense when daylight broke through the haze of night. He snuggled closer to Abby and his cock slid against her folds. He gritted his teeth. It was all he could do to not take this woman now and make her his.

Why did he want her so badly?

Abby made a soft sigh and turned in his arms so that she was facing him. Her eyelids fluttered open and her jaw dropped open in shock. She tried to jerk away from him but he held her too tightly.

"You—I thought…" Abby closed her eyes tight. "A dream. This is all a dream."

Kir gave a soft laugh and caught her chin in his hand. "This is no dream, kitten. You are in Oz and you now belong to me."

With that Abby's eyes flew open. She braced her arms on his chest and tried to push away. But he held her firmly with his arms and his thigh pinning her hips. His cock jutted against her belly and her breasts were pressed against his chest.

She stopped fighting and her tongue flicked out to wet her bottom lip. Her cinnamon eyes darkened and he could scent her arousal. So easy…it would be so easy to take her now.

But no. She needed to be taught her place in his world.

He released her and pushed himself to his feet. An expression of confusion and disappointment crossed her fae features, followed by anger.

She scrambled to stand and almost fell against the emerald wall of his chambers. He caught her by one arm to steady her but she jerked away from him and glared.

"Your punishments mount." He darkened his expression even though he found her spirit…adorable. There could be no other word for it.

Abby folded her arms across her chest. "This is bullshit. I am an American and I'm free to do what I choose."

Kir shook his head. "Whoever you were, that identity has come to an end. You are a subject of Oz now. And you will bow to my authority."

She balled her fists at her sides. "Like hell."

"You seem to have forgotten your punishment last night," Kir said in a warning tone. "That was light compared to what you will face if this resistance continues."

Abby's body tensed and she glanced around the room as if looking for a way to escape. "I can't believe this is happening to me." She faced him and tilted up her chin. "What will it take for you to send me home?"

"This is your home." He kept his voice as stern as possible. "And you will start by referring to me as M'Lord. Immediately." He held out his hand and the handle of a leather whip appeared in his palm. "You will also keep your gaze lowered, your chest thrust forward, your hands behind your back and your stance wide whenever you are around me. And you will never climax without my permission."

Abby's eyes widened as he spoke. She opened her mouth, looked at the flogger and shut her mouth again. Darkness flickered through her features, momentarily hiding the light of her spirit. Kir frowned.

What was he seeing?

Was he misjudging something about her?

Before he could identify the source of his disquiet, Abby dropped her gaze, took the position he had ordered her to assume and grumbled, "Yes, M'Lord." And what he thought was *asshole* under her breath. He chose to ignore that and began walking around her.

She was exquisite. From her small breasts and high nipples, to her slender curves and rounded ass. He loved her fae features, the way her auburn hair tumbled over her shoulders, and the sprinkling of faerie kisses across her nose and shoulders.

More than wanting to train her to their mutual pleasure, more than wanting to assert his absolute alpha authority, he wanted to *please* her. Show her delights she had never let herself imagine.

If I am not cautious she will steal away my soul faster than any bakir. *By the gods, I do not understand my own feelings.*

But despite his confusion, he was a Lord and a lover, with a very challenging subject to train. He had to keep control of himself.

When he returned to face her, he ran the whip over his hand. "You do realize that you must be punished for your numerous infractions of my rules, do you not?"

"Yes, M'Lord," Abby said with a sigh.

"Good. You may raise your eyes." The spark of defiance in her gaze almost made him smile. "After breakfast I will show you my realm. Your punishments will follow."

At his mental command, servants entered his quarters and placed a meal upon a table at which two chairs were situated. The delicious smells of the food rose to meet him and he heard Abby's stomach growl as she sat at the table, naked and beautiful as always. After scooting closer to the table, she filled her plate and ate bread and strips of roasted meat. She also sampled other delicacies of his realm. At times she would frown or grimace, but she seemed too intent on devouring her meal to speak.

She has the appetite of a weretiger too. Some day, she will likely be great friends with the Queens of Tarok. If I am ever addled enough to let them meet, that is.

A mental image of one of the Queens, Alexi of Spades, mate of King Darronn, formed quite clearly. If those two got together, they might well overtake both kingdoms and lock the kings in their dungeons for a change.

Kir shifted uncomfortably thinking of how much Darronn had to sacrifice to win his mate. How much Darronn had to *compromise*.

Well, that would not happen to him.

He would have this woman, Abby, and he would have her on his terms.

And by the nineteen hells of his people, he would *not* think of King Darronn and Queen Alexi again.

When they finished eating Kir took Abby by the hand and helped her to her feet. "Come, kitten. I shall show you Oz."

"Yes, M'Lord," Abby said, but it sounded like she was grinding her teeth as it came through her lips. "But can I put on clothing, please?"

"No."

She sighed but didn't argue.

O greeted them at the door as they left his chambers. The dog's tail twitched as he yipped a greeting. Abby fell to her knees and gathered the animal into her arms. "Hey, boy, I've missed you." She raised a brow in Kir's direction. "Bite anyone recently, O?"

"Release the beast and rise," demanded Kir, feeling unreasonably jealous of the pet, then feeling stupid over that, then angry over feeling stupid—all in a matter of seconds.

He had to shake his head to clear his senses.

Seemingly unaware of his reactions, Abby rose, gathered the leash hooked to O's collar and pulled him to her side. "But can't he go with us?" Her bottom lip pushed out like a disappointed child and that fast he went from frustrated to confused to charmed.

In fact he had to hold back a grin.

She *was* adorable. Kir didn't have the strength to deny her. "Yes, if you can keep him restrained." Her smile lit the room, dying quickly when he added, "And you must obey me or I will send him back."

It was time to explore his city.

Soon Abby's defiance turned to wonder as she took in the sights. The emerald cavern itself was beautiful with its waterfall and the green glow that touched everything. There were stalagmites and stalactites but underground flowers and soft mossy grass provided places for his people to relax and enjoy the falls — and the pleasures of the flesh.

Abby turned a pretty shade of pink when she saw three men fucking one woman. The enraptured woman sat astride one man, riding his cock, while a second thrust in and out of her ass and a third drove in and out of her mouth. Moans of ecstasy floated on the air, not only from the quartet, but from other couples and ménages in various places in the large cavern. As his was a Dominant and submissive society, many subs were being erotically punished. Kir did not allow cruelty of any kind so he knew that the partners engaged in bondage and submission were always willing.

Kir slipped behind Abby and murmured in her ear, "Would you like to be fucked like that woman?"

She visibly swallowed. "N-no, M'Lord."

"Liar." He nipped at her lobe and felt her shudder of desire. "You agreed to submit because you truly want to be dominated. I can sense it, Abby. Don't try to lie to me." He bit her lobe harder this time and she gave a soft cry. "Tell me, do you enjoy being dominated? Giving up control?"

Abby groaned and turned toward him so that his lips brushed her cheek. "Yes, M'Lord," she whispered a second before his lips possessed hers.

The kiss was so intense it made Kir's head spin. He wanted to take Abby down to the mossy ground and claim her for all to see. And he knew she would love it. Would revel in it.

When Kir thought he would lose control, he pulled away from Abby and straightened. She looked up at him with desire-filled eyes that almost undid him. Gods, she was sweet and she craved him surely as much as he craved her.

He took Abby away from the large chamber into another large one that was lined with shops. Warm smells of fresh baked breads and fruit tarts filled the air from the baker's, along with rich scents of roasted meat from the butcher's. O jerked against his leash looking as though he wanted to investigate the smells, but Abby kept him by her side.

Kir's people chose to live a combination of the human life and lupine life. Their primal urges often sent them roaming the lands as wolves, tracking animals for food and devouring the meat in the wilds.

But this was a place where his people could choose to barter wares for their individual caves, their homes. There were jewelers, clothiers, toymakers and many other types of shops. Children and wolf pups alike scampered in and out of the crowds of people, most naked like the adults, something that was very natural to his people.

Children were never allowed in the pleasure spots of the underground city, but did run freely in the common areas.

"It's like being in the lobby of a huge hotel." Abby's eyes were wide and sparkling as she looked around, obviously absorbing everything she saw. "Shops of every kind. I just never imagined something like this could exist underground."

Due to her excitement and enthusiasm Kir ignored the fact that she had forgotten to refer to him as "M'Lord." This time.

As always, his people bowed to him as he passed, in deference to him being their Alpha, Lord of the cave-dwelling mountain wolves. He noticed too their curious glances at Abby. It was obvious by her scent that she was not of their kind.

When they passed a jeweler's, Abby stopped in front of the sandglass and her jaw dropped. "Ohmigod." She said the words in one long rush as she pointed to one of the larger diamonds that glittered with the brilliance of a thousand shards of sunlight. "That would probably be worth several million dollars back home."

"Would you like it?" he asked.

Abby's gaze shot to his. "You're kidding, right?"

He fixed his eyes on hers. "Not at all."

She shook her head as she studied the diamond again, her auburn hair brushing her naked back. "No way. That would be like carrying a golf ball on your finger." She looked up at him again. "Besides, I'm a country girl. I like simple things."

Kir stroked his knuckles across her cheek. "You are a fair maiden who deserves the most exquisite finery."

Abby caught her breath and their eyes locked for one long moment. She visibly swallowed then turned her gaze back to the jewels on display. Rings, earrings, nipple rings, necklaces, bracelets. Everything a woman or man could want. Her gaze settled on a glittering pair of ruby and diamond earrings but she shook her head. "Not for me."

While they explored the shops, Kir found himself looking at his realm through Abby's appreciative gaze. He had taken for granted what had been here for hundreds of years. She, however, exclaimed her delight over the network of tunnels and homes built right into the cavern for all his people.

When they were hungry Kir had one of the storekeepers prepare them a picnic lunch and he took Abby to the main cavern to sit by the waterfall and watch the colorful fish swimming beneath its clear surface. A fine mist coated Kir's and Abby's naked flesh as they settled on the mossy carpet. The air smelled of fresh water, underground orchids and their meal of roasted fish and baked vegetables. But above it all, Abby's womanly scent was driving him crazy. He'd controlled his erection while he was amongst his people, but now it was almost beyond his management. He wanted Abby and he wanted her now.

While they ate, O munching happily on a bone, Abby studied their surroundings. Her face was almost a permanent shade of pink from seeing all the couplings in the cavern. She did her best to avoid looking directly at them, but when they were finished eating, Kir caught her chin in one of his hands.

"Look." With his guidance he pointed her gaze directly at a man and woman. The woman was being fucked from behind by a man who was spanking her ass, causing it to be bright pink. "Would you like to be taken like that?"

Abby blushed as bright of a shade of pink as the woman's ass. She glanced up at him and visibly swallowed.

"Do not lie to me." Kir's voice was a low warning. "I will know."

"Yes." Abby trembled beneath his touch. "I want to be fucked like that."

Kir's cock swelled to unbelievable proportions but he kept his voice calm. "You have been forgetting something very important, wench. And that is how you are to refer to me."

Abby's nose crinkled and then she said with a roll of her eyes, "Yeah. M'Lord. I'm supposed to call you that."

He gave her a rigid frown that caused her to pull away from his touch. "It is time for you to take your punishments."

"Oh, shit." Abby looked nervous and licked her lips. "Jeez. Did you really mean all that? Look I'm not even from around here. I don't belong here and I'm not sure I want to be a part of any of this."

"M'Lord."

A flash of fire lit her eyes. "Yeah, M'Lord. Right."

Anger burned low in the pit of his stomach as he grabbed her hands and pulled her to her feet. O immediately came to her side. "You belong to me now, and you will accept your position in my world."

She jerked away from him and placed her hands on her hips. "Bullshit."

With a low growl Kir grabbed Abby around the waist and slung her over his shoulder. She yelped as he flung her so that her pussy was against his shoulder, her breasts against his back, her long hair caressing his ass.

"Oooooh! Let me down, you big—big—Neanderthal!"

Kir slapped her ass and she yelped again.

"Come, O," he commanded. The dog followed, his leash trailing.

Well. At least the beast obeys me.

Kir ignored the covert glances of his people as he passed by them and headed toward his private dungeon. The fact that anyone had ignored his orders, had talked back to him, was unheard of. He was Lord of the Realm.

Abby's potential host of sarcastic responses echoed in his mind.

What did Neanderthal mean? He was certain it wasn't a proper way to address her Lord.

"Your punishments will be far more serious if you insult me again," he said through clenched teeth.

Abby's response was to bite his ass.

Kir roared. With his magic he flung open the doors to his dungeon. "Stay," he bellowed to the pet.

O came to an abrupt halt and sat.

Kir shut the doors behind them with a crash, barring the heavy wooden structures with his powers. He strode to the center of the room where a cage was situated. It was made of emerald bars, only long enough for a woman to be on her hands and knees, which was exactly where he intended Abby to be.

He slipped her down his length, holding back the groan that wanted to issue from behind his teeth just from the feel of his cock against her fair skin. He placed his hands on her shoulders and forced her to her knees. "In the cage, wench."

"Bite me," she said with fury in her eyes.

He held out his hand and a whip soared through the air from its place upon the wall of instruments used to punish subs.

The moment he had it in his hand, Abby looked at it, looked at the ferocious expression on his face, dropped to her knees and crawled into the cage. He let the whip fall to the floor and summoned another instrument of torture from the wall, one that would make Abby crazy with the need to climax but unable to come.

Crouching on his knees, he reached into the cage and slipped the dildo into her wet pussy. With each movement he made Abby moaned and shuddered.

When the dildo was held in place by his magic, he slammed the cage door behind her.

Abby winced.

Kir walked to the front of the cage and motioned for her to move closer to him as he pushed his erection through the bars. "Pleasure me," he demanded.

She looked as though she wanted to bite off his cock and he almost thought better of his plan.

She wouldn't dare.

Would she?

Just as he broke a sweat wondering, she moved closer to him and scooted so that she was on her haunches. No doubt her movements deepened the feel of the dildo that was designed to expand within her, to fill her, but also to not allow her to climax.

The moment she slipped her lips over his staff Kir almost let loose with a groan. He grabbed her hair through the bars and began fucking her mouth the way he wanted to drive into her wet heat. She didn't fight him. Instead she took him deep, swirling her tongue along his length while bringing her hand up and working his cock in tandem with her mouth. The way she moaned and closed her eyes it was obvious she was getting pleasure from his size, his taste.

The thought drove him to new heights.

When he came it was fast, furious and unexpected. He couldn't help the shout that echoed through the dungeon. His cock pulsed inside her warmth and his orgasm went on and on for a long, sweet moment. She kept her eyes focused on him as she sucked, drawing his fluid down her throat.

Mind dull from the release, feeling like he had a fist around his heart, Kir pulled his cock from the stubborn woman's mouth.

At least he still had a cock. That might be counted as progress.

As for what she did to him, the way his body responded to her touch…

Once more the image of King Darronn besotted with love for his fire-breathing off-world wife tortured Kir's mind.

I am not Darronn, he told himself firmly. *I will not surrender my heart to any woman, least of all this one. I'd be a fool…*

But didn't true love make a fool of any man, weretiger or werewolf, four-legged or two?

Damn the fates.

Here he was, standing next to the cage of his uncooperative submissive, already erect again at just the thought of fucking Abby.

He would not.

He would keep control of himself. He would deny her pleasure for as long as possible until she realized she belonged to him.

There was no other way to tame her.

If she can be tamed.

Chapter Ten

ဢ

Abby knew she was going out of her mind.

Days had passed—over a week—and all Kir would do was erotically torture her, bringing her close to the brink of orgasm, only to deny her again and again. The more she defied him, the more he made her need to climax. And she didn't know how he was preventing her from reaching the zenith. She was hardly ever alone—so masturbation was out. While she was with him it was as if she needed his touch to stroke the fire inside her. It was maddening and beyond frustrating.

And she loved everything he did to her. It didn't make sense. She hated him one moment for making her crazy with need. Then in the next, she was experiencing such pleasure from his spankings, his floggings, that she didn't want them to end.

She thought often of Balin and his offer to help her escape.

And what about Aunt Maye? Did her aunt wonder what happened to her? Was she grieving? God, Abby hoped the elderly woman was all right.

Abby was sure she was losing her mind as her next thought came—*do I really want to leave Oz?*

Right now all she wanted to do was come.

Again she had awakened in Kir's arms, teased into awareness by the most exquisite feel of skin against skin. Her eyes opened and Kir lay spooned into her back as usual. His erection was tucked between her thighs, her moist heat immediately anointing him. She moved her hips, rubbing her folds across his cock.

The way he held her made Abby feel safe, wanted. One hand cupped her breast, the other wrapped around her waist. They were so close even air didn't come between them.

Abby reached between her legs and stroked the head of his shaft as her hips continued to move back and forth. He hardened even more and greeted her teasing fingers with pre-come. His juices were slick as she spread them over the crown of his erection.

"You're playing with fire." His growl filtered through her. He squeezed her nipple and lightning shot through her breast.

"I don't mind getting burned, M'Lord," she purred. She could feel his heartbeat quicken against her back. Maybe he would take her. This time he would drive into her and let her scream her release.

He moved away from her and rose. She turned on her back and watched him disappear behind the rock wall.

When Kir returned he wore a pair of tight, black leather pants. And they didn't look too comfortable. The man was aroused just as much as she was, and still he refused both of them a moment of pleasure.

Damn the man.

"Rise, Abby," he demanded. "Linara approaches."

Now how the hell did he know that? But just as she finished the thought, the door opened and Linara stepped inside.

The dark-haired woman bowed. The hungry expression she flashed Kir set Abby on edge.

"M'Lord," Linara cooed. "You have need of me?" There was a world of insinuation in her words.

"Escort Abby to the ocean. I need to meet with Janan."

"As you wish, M'Lord." She bowed again.

Kir walked over to Abby and extended his hand. She accepted it and rose to her feet. As he took her into his arms, his erection pressed against the leather of his pants and felt hard next to her stomach. She bent her knees, working her body up and down, teasing his cock through his breeches.

He growled and bit her neck. She jumped and couldn't help a small giggle. Then he kissed her.

God, what a kiss.

When they broke apart he continued to hold her, his mouth next to her ear. "Remember you cannot escape me, my kitten. Any attempts will be dealt with swiftly." He released her, pivoted, and left the room.

Linara drifted toward the exit. "Come, M'Lady."

"I wish," Abby muttered as she followed the woman down a hall and then another corridor.

She hesitated, her gaze scanning the area for escape routes.

Why am I doing this? Do I really want to get away?

Of course she did. What would it say about her sanity if she wanted to stay?

Damn it. I should at least get one mind-blowing orgasm out of the bargain, shouldn't I?

At the intersection where she stood there were four archways, three of which she was now familiar with. The emerald one she had just come from, a diamond one, an archway trimmed with rubies and one of sapphires. Linara was heading through the ruby archway.

Deciding there would be a better opportunity to get away, Abby hurried to join the woman. She noted that the hallway had a slight grade to it. They were headed upwards. "Where's O?" she asked.

"He is being fed in one of the kitchens," Linara said.

When the light of day brushed Abby's face, a sense of freedom shook her. She hadn't known how much she loved the outdoors, loved the earth. Farming had been a drudge, but evidently had meant a lot to her and had formed who she was more than she had realized. She'd been underground over a week and it felt damn good to be outside. She was bummed that O couldn't join them right now. He'd love it out here.

The one thing that puzzled Abby were her continuing dreams of Balin. Nightly he called to her, promised to free her from bondage, reminding her to pretend to surrender to Kir. But when she awoke she was certain it was simply a dream.

And she didn't have to pretend to submit to Kir. She craved it.

But what she really needed was her freedom. Yes, that's what she wanted. Wasn't it?

In the distance an ocean curled in and out to hug and release the shore. Emerald green waters flowed across shimmering white sand. Lord Kir's mountain was behind her. Rich, verdant forest lay on each side of his kingdom and seemed to disappear into the waters. She turned to examine the cave she had just exited but it wasn't there. Instead a vast landscape of greenery and flowers of every shape, size and color hid the entrance. Her gaze followed a little path carved into the side of earth until the tip of the mountain disappeared among the blue-green clouds lingering in the sky.

"It's so beautiful," Abby murmured. Apparently they had taken a backdoor out of the mountain. She hadn't even realized the ocean was near when Kir had dragged her back to Emerald City. Perhaps it was due to it being blocked by the mountain and forest on two sides.

"Emerald City, as well as Lord Kir, is cherished among all the kingdoms in the realm," Linara said as they walked down the embankment.

Abby snorted.

The woman stopped heading toward the waters and turned to face her. "Are you not pleased that you have been chosen to mate with Lord Kir?"

"Mate? I'm not a friggin' animal. I choose who I fuck and who I don't."

Linara looked puzzled. "It is an honor to lay with the Lord of the cave-dwelling mountain wolves. Do you not wish to be his queen, bear his pups?"

The idea was absurd. Abby pressed a palm to her abdomen. "Hell, no. I just want to go home." After she fucked him and after she had what was bound to be an incredible orgasm after all this wait.

Damn it, if it was the last thing she did she would get him to fuck her.

As they came to a rock table laden with what smelled like food, Abby's stomach growled. The woman smiled. "Perhaps you need to attend to other needs first." Linara waved Abby over to a clump of bushes.

She had forgotten to use the bathroom before they left. Evidently this wondrous outdoors didn't have the comfort features of a bathroom or even an outhouse. Well, it wasn't like Abby hadn't relieved herself behind the bushes before. Sand shifted beneath her feet as she strode up the rise and disappeared among the hedges. As she slipped into the greenery, a flock of frightened birds tore across the sky. Beautiful blue and magenta feathers covered the strange little creatures that looked like a cross between a parrot and an owl.

When she finished taking care of her needs, she moved to the water's edge and crouched on the wet sand to wash her hands.

Something glistening off the surface caught her eye as she shook the water from her hands. It was a man swimming in the water — the same man who had butt-fucked Linara the day Abby had arrived. Eral. Yeah, that was his name.

As he cut through the whitecaps, the look of rapture on Eral's face was entrancing. His hair was like thick threads of silver that gave the illusion of moonbeams as it flowed like a cape behind him.

A large tailfin slapped the water behind him. Another appeared, hitting the surface hard, spewing a fountain of water high into the air. Eral's head disappeared beneath the emerald green water.

Abby sprang to her feet. Her heart thrashed against her chest. When the man reappeared she sucked in a breath as a ring of dorsal fins appeared and began to circle Eral. She waited for his expression of fear. Instead, he only grinned.

"Sharks!" Abby screamed. She began to jump up and down waving her arms. "Sharks. Get out of the water. Swim!"

When the man's head dipped beneath the surface and disappeared again, Abby's heart nearly stopped beating.

She started screaming. "Linara! The sharks ate Eral!"

"M'lady." A deep rumbling voice shocked Abby so badly she screamed again. Eral strode out of the water before her, a very naked Eral, who caressed her bare flesh with his strange blue gaze. A boyish grin was plastered on his face as he winked.

In the bend of his elbow he held what looked like a sealskin that sparkled with the colors of a rainbow. Following him were four more men just exiting the water, each carrying similar pelts. Eral raised his free hand and all the hides disappeared into thin air.

Eral reached for her arm, which hung limply by her side. Goose bumps rose across her flesh as his warm touch slid down her arm until he grasped her hand. Eyes pinned on hers, he slowly turned her hand palm up and then he pressed his lips against her wrist.

Her nipples tightened and she sucked in her breath

He smiled at her reaction and bowed low. "Until later," Eral purred.

Yeow! Yes. No. Not later. Now.

Kir popped into her mind, and her desires simmered down to nothing.

What the hell?

It wasn't like she *only* wanted that bastard.

Was it?

But what about the sharks? How did these men survive? Where did the pelts come from, not to mention, where did they disappear to? Abby scanned the water's surface. All evidence of the sharks was gone.

She watched Eral's tight, naked ass and those of his friends as they walked away. Hubba, hubba. Momma needed to get her a few of those.

When Abby felt Linara's presence beside her she turned. "Did you see that? Those men survived shark-infested waters."

Linara cocked her head, a bewildered expression rose. "Sharks?"

"Man-eating fish."

Laughter drifted sweetly from the woman's lips. "Nothing in these waters would harm Prince Eral and his people."

"Prince?" The man was a prince?

"Come. You must be hungry." As Abby followed her, Linara explained. "Prince Eral is a werefin, where Lord Kir and our people are werewolves."

Abby stopped short in her steps. "You mean he's a fish?"

Again soft laughter met Abby's confusion. "No, he is a werefin."

In high school Abby had taken a class on Celtic Mythology. She remembered a legendary race that shed their sealskins and took the form of humans. They were known to have magical seduction powers, which she didn't doubt Eral had.

"A selkie?" she whispered in awe.

"I do not know this word selkie, but Prince Eral's kingdom is beneath the waters."

"Then why is he here with Lord Kir's clan?"

"M'Lord rescued the prince's mother from an evil sorcerer," Linara said. "Prince Eral has remained in Lord Kir's debt since then. Until the debt is paid, Prince Eral refuses to return to his family, his rightful throne."

This world was just too freaking weird.

Yet Abby couldn't resist asking, "Linara, what's it like to fuck a werefin?"

A smug expression filtered over Linara's face. "His magical seed in a woman's body does many wondrous things."

"The colors." Abby's jaw dropped as it dawned on her. "Your body changed colors."

"Yes, but do you not wonder why?" The look of ecstasy on Linara's face made Abby's breasts grow heavy.

Oh yeah, Abby had wondered why the woman's body had flashed several different hues when she climaxed. Abby had also wondered what it felt like to be fucked by two men at the same time. Even three. After what she'd seen in the cavern on many occasions, her imagination had soared.

Yet that stubborn part of her brain kept getting stuck on Kir.

This was really ridiculous, considering that all he did was torture her. And the fact that he was keeping her prisoner.

Eral's parting words, "Until later," rang in Abby's ears. Moisture was quick to dampen her thighs. Well, hot damn! She was going to have fish tonight. Maybe Eral would let her come at least.

Then she thought of Kir again.

The werefin's appeal faded.

Okay, so I'm insane, but I think I have to have Kir at least once. First. Then all bets are off.

Chapter Eleven

ᔕᓄ

Balin lightly stroked the crystal ball as he gazed into it. His long black hair drifted over his shoulders as he narrowed his eyes.

"Where is my pretty now?" he murmured as mist swirled through the crystal globe. The fog danced and whirled, then slowly bled away until he saw the naked auburn beauty on the shores of the north side of Kir's realm.

He gritted his teeth and clenched his fist above the globe. Muscles flexed in his powerful chest and biceps as fury rocked him. If Kir's scouts had not found his *bakirs*, they would be in position to snatch Abby of Kansas this very minute and bring her to Malachad.

Balin's mouth twisted into a cruel smile as he watched Abby stare out at the sea. Her self-confidence was wavering and she was weakening from his nightly visits to her dreams. Soon she would be his.

His cock rose at the thought of taking her, strapping her to the stretching bars in his torture chamber and fucking her while Lord Kir watched. Kir would be in chains, against the wall, bound so tightly and drugged so well that he could never escape or shift into a wolf. But he would remember every minute of his torture. And Abby would love Balin's touch far more than the werewolf's.

The sorcerer started to take his hand away from the crystal ball and mist began to swirl within it once more. He paused, spread his fingers wide over the globe, and it cleared again.

Fury caused Balin to tremble as that bastard of a prince, Eral, stood before Abby, obviously reeking of the sea. He couldn't help but hear Abby's thoughts, feel her burst of lust for the werefin that died when she thought of Lord Kir.

Balin's fingers trembled. He wanted to slit the prince's throat so badly he could taste the coppery essence of blood on his tongue.

Why was his world so thick with interfering betrayers?

Thanks to the brothers of Tarok, their mates, and Kir, he had lost Mikaela, the only one strong enough to control all the *bakirs* and defeat the four kings.

He had lost the only woman he had ever loved.

The bitch had unraveled his plans with the help of Tarok's sorceress, Kalina. His mindspell had been broken. His power had been weakened.

Fury shook him that Mikaela even now evaded his reach. Yes, when he found the Tarok kings' sister—his faithless wife and ex-queen—she would die a very slow and painful death. The bitch Kalina would be his to torture as well.

Now that Tarok was lost to him, Balin intended to have Kir's Emerald City.

And next would be Eral's Kingdom of Atlantis.

The corner of his mouth curved into a wicked grin as he rubbed his golden ring and he gave a soft laugh.

Abby was the key. Yes, he had felt the loneliness in the air around Lord Kir. The wolf would not be whole without his mate. Already his adversary had grown to think of the woman as his. Their bond—connection—was already beginning to ease the unrest within the man.

Balin rubbed his palms together feeling the heat of success build. Soon she would be his. His tongue made a savory path along his bottom lip.

And the best thing was that the wolf's mate would come to Balin freely and give herself into his captivity. His grin deepened.

Abby of Kansas would be the ruin of them all.

Chapter Twelve

🔊

Lord Kir folded his arms across his broad chest as he stood within the edges of his forest. Despite what he had planned with Eral, Abby and Linara, a fierce sense of possessiveness caused him to clench his teeth as the prince spoke with Abby on the beach. She was to be *his* packmate. And right now he didn't want to share her with anyone.

Abby was exquisite. Red highlighted her hair, and her fae features were so delicate. Her eyes and expression held warmth as she spoke with Eral, warmth she had rarely shown Kir.

He growled beneath his breath as the prince said something low, his eyes caressing Abby from head to toe. Eral departed and a wicked smile crossed Abby's beautiful features.

A smile that churned Kir's gut. It was obvious she would find great pleasure in sex with the werefin. A thought that did not settle well with Kir.

Gods, it seemed as if it had been months since the beauty had come into his life rather than a good week. She touched him in ways that amazed him. One moment he wanted to hold her close and love her and the next he wanted to throttle her.

Kir strode out of the forest, onto the beach. The sand was warm beneath his bare feet and the breeze off the ocean cool against his naked flesh.

Abby whipped her gaze from Eral's retreating back to meet Kir's eyes. A guilty look flashed across her expression but it quickly vanished.

"M'Lord," Linara said, drawing his attention to the black-haired beauty. "What may I do to serve you?"

Her eyes were downcast, her hands behind her back, the stones on her necklace glistening in the sunlight.

"Leave us," Kir said more curtly than he'd intended.

If his sharp words had affected Linara, she did not show it. She simply bowed, said "Yes, M'Lord," and retreated toward the entrance to Emerald City.

When Kir cut his gaze to Abby, she was staring at him with that ever-present defiant look in her cinnamon eyes. He almost smiled at the spirit she showed. Instead he forced himself to frown. Her gaze lowered to the sand and she moved her hands behind her back, but he swore he saw her stick her middle finger out as she did it.

He almost laughed. "Come," he said, holding back his amusement at his feisty wench. "You will eat with me."

"Whatever," he thought he heard her mumble under her breath.

He reached her in three strides. He hooked his finger under her chin and raised it so that her head was tipped back and her eyes met his.

Her expression of defiance melted and her tongue darted out to touch her upper lip. Instead of antagonism in her gaze, desire burned hot and strong.

He captured her face in both his strong hands and crushed his lips to hers. She opened for him at once, her moans becoming increasingly frantic as he plundered her hot mouth. Taking from her, demanding of her, possessing her.

She pressed her small body to his and he couldn't hold back his groan at the feel of her taut nipples rubbing his chest, her small, firm body snug against him. His erection prodded her belly and he wanted only to take her down to the sand and fuck her until she screamed to be allowed to come.

But something bothered him that he didn't want to acknowledge. Something that made him hesitate.

He wanted more from Abby than her submission.

Kir's gut burned with the knowledge of the truth.

He wanted this woman's heart and soul.

When he tore his mouth from hers, it took all of his control not to reveal how she had affected him. Her cinnamon eyes had turned a rich shade of mahogany, dark with desire, her breathing ragged. Her chest rose and fell, her nipples brushing his chest and driving him out of his mind.

Instead of commanding her, he took her hand and tugged her near the water's edge, toward the table laden with breakfast foods. "Come," he said in a gentle tone.

Abby looked surprised but said only, "Yes, M'Lord."

A large emerald-green blanket spread across the sand beneath the squat table. Kir lowered himself and crossed his legs, then pulled Abby into his lap.

She gave a little yelp of surprise and then a soft moan as his raging erection pressed to her ass. He gritted his teeth against the desire to plunge into her now. Instead, he concentrated on teaching her true pleasure.

He arranged her so that she sat sideways in his lap and he could see her breasts and the spark in her eyes.

Smiling, he raised his hand and brushed his fingers over the faerie kisses across her nose and cheeks.

She wrinkled her nose. "My freckles. I know they're awful. Er, M'Lord."

He gave her a stern look. "Your faerie kisses are most beautiful. Never say otherwise."

Her eyes widened. "Yes, M'Lord."

He dipped his head to press his lips to a cluster of faerie kisses below one of her eyes. Her lashes fluttered shut and she snuggled her ass between his thighs so that his cock was pressed hard against her hip.

Kir raised his head and reached for one of the delicacies on the table. He brought it to her lips and she opened her eyes.

"May I speak, M'Lord?" she asked.

"Freely now," he said and she gave a sigh that had her breasts rising and falling.

"What the hell is this?" She pointed to the wafer and the pink spread upon it.

He wasn't sure she would want to know exactly what it was. "Taste."

She opened her mouth as if to respond but he slipped the wafer into her mouth. She paused, then took a small bite and chewed. He held the remainder and almost laughed as her mouth puckered. "Damn, that's sour!"

"But good, yes?"

Abby tilted her head to the side and her long hair slid over his arm like a caress. "Yeah. It's all right." She leaned forward and he fed her the rest of the wafer.

Her stomach growled and she glanced up at him. "I guess it's pretty good."

He inclined his head toward the table. "Feed me."

Abby glanced at the spread and chose a piece of red *lini* fruit. "Can I ask you anything?" she said as she brought the fruit to his lips and slipped it into his mouth. He caught her finger with his teeth and sucked it as he slowly released it. Abby shuddered and goose bumps erupted over her skin.

"Yes," he said after he finished chewing the delicious morsel. "You may ask anything of me." He reached for a piece of *lini* to feed Abby.

She eyed him straight on. "When can I go home?"

Of all the questions, he should have expected that one but he hadn't. He gave her a stern look. "You know you belong to me now. There is no returning to this Kanzaz you spoke of. That isn't possible. Even if it were, I would not allow it."

Abby clenched one fist on the table. "We'll see about that."

In a movement so fast that a cry of shock spilled from her lips, Kir had Abby pinned to the blanket, beneath him. He braced his arms to either side of her head. She stared up at him with her eyes wide, her palms braced against his chest.

"Mine." He let out another low growl, fighting the change to his more feral wolf form. "Mine."

He forced his hips between her thighs and pressed his cock to her belly. Abby's breath caught, her lips parted, and he dove for her luscious mouth. He thrust his tongue within her warmth at the same time he pumped his hips against hers.

With a soft moan, she slid her hands from his chest to around his neck and wrapped her thighs around his hips. "Fuck me." Her breath was warm against his lips when their mouths parted. "Please fuck me."

"When you have earned it, wench." He lowered his head and his long hair slid over her chest as his mouth took possession of one of her nipples.

She clenched her hands in his hair and squirmed beneath him. "Have you gone Dom on me again?"

"The time to speak freely has ended." He bit her nipple and she cried out.

"Yes, M'Lord!"

Kir knew she was close to orgasm already and again he had to use the powers of his mind to ensure she did not reach climax until he was ready for her to.

He bit Abby's other nipple and she pulled his hair so hard that the pain and pleasure of it rippled through him. He licked and sucked each nipple, then bit the ultra-sensitive nubs until Abby's body shuddered. So close. Dangerously close.

"Remember, wench." He moved his mouth close to her ear. "You are not allowed to reach orgasm without my permission."

"Fuck y—" she started, then said, "Yes, M'Lord," in a voice that told him she was furious at him for making her wait. After over a week of being forced to refrain from climax, he was certain that her punishment was nearly fulfilled.

When he nipped at her lower lip, she moaned and squirmed, her body begging for more.

Kir moved his lips down the curve of her neck, kissing and licking a trail along the faerie kisses on her shoulders, to the hollow of her throat. "You are so lovely." He pressed his lips between her breasts. "So very lovely."

"You're not so bad yourself," she said then hurried to add, "M'Lord."

He suppressed a chuckle. "Did I give you leave to speak, wench?"

"No, M'Lord."

He straddled her, his knees to either side of her chest, and grabbed both her breasts. He slid his cock between the soft mounds and slowly began to fuck her breasts at the same time he pinched her nipples. Hard.

Abby gasped and arched her back. Her eyes rolled back as she released his hair to clench her hands in the blanket to either side of her.

"Your nipples. The luscious color of starflower blooms." He pressed her breasts harder together around his cock. "Raise your head."

She did as he instructed and his erection was so great that it reached her lips as he slid in and out of her soft mounds. "Lick my cock."

Abby's tongue laved the engorged head of his erection. Hot. Wet. It took all he had to suppress his groans of pleasure.

When he came too close to climax, he released her breasts to explore more of her body.

The sun was warm on his back as he moved to kneel between her thighs. The crash of waves against shore matched the pounding of his heart. In the forest he heard the whisper of wind through trees and the howl of one of his scouts indicating that all was clear.

But what truly occupied his attention was the woman beneath him. Perspiration coated her skin, but he knew it had nothing to do with the warmth of the sun. Her breathing was shallow and her nipples and breasts red, swollen and aching from his mouth and his hands. "Wherever I touch you," he murmured as he traced his finger from one faerie kiss to the next on her chest, "your soft skin turns such a beautiful color of pink."

Abby simply looked up at him with lust-filled eyes.

He lowered his head and started to kiss a path between her breasts. "What would you have me do now?" he asked as he trailed his tongue down to her navel and neared her mound.

By now she clenched the emerald green blanket so tightly her knuckles were as white as the sand. "Lick my pussy. Please, M'Lord."

Kir nuzzled her soft curls. "If it pleases me."

Abby groaned.

"Your scent…" He inhaled deeply. "Gods, you smell so good. The sweet perfume of woman, yet distinctly a scent all your own."

Abby moaned and raised her hips, showing him how badly she wanted him to lick her quim.

He sniffed again and nuzzled her folds, teasing her, making her wait. "Yes, I need to taste you."

Kir buried his mouth within Abby's folds. She cried out and bucked her hips against his face.

He rose and gave her a firm look. "Do not come, wench."

"Please, M'Lord." Abby's voice trembled. "I'm so close."

"You must learn control." He lowered his head again and licked her hard button.

"Oh, god." Abby's eyes were wide and she thrashed her head from side to side. "Ohgod. Ohgod. Ohgod."

"I must say," he said as he swiped his tongue against her clit again, "I've been called many things, but never a deity."

"Conceited bastard," Abby mumbled under her breath.

When he raised his head she flushed. "You have earned a punishment, wench." He moved one finger to her folds and plunged it up to his knuckles in her channel. "Would you like to be tied up in my bed as punishment?"

"If you fuck me while I'm there." Abby bit her lower lip. "I mean no, M'Lord."

The image of having Abby tied in his bed, stretched wide for his pleasure, was strong enough to make Kir have to bite his tongue to keep from growling his passion aloud. "I will find a suitable punishment for you, wench."

He frowned as her eyes glittered like they often had in the dungeon, a spark that seemed to say, "Yes, please!"

Kir licked her quim unmercifully, all the while using his mind-control to ensure she would not climax. Abby thrashed and cried out, shoving her folds against his mouth and squirming beneath him.

"Damn it!" Tears rolled down her face, she was so in need of climax. "It's been over a week. Let me come, M'Lord, *please*."

Kir bit her clit and she screamed loud enough to startle *eloin* birds from the forest trees. It took all his power to keep her from climaxing.

"M'Lord," she sobbed. "You're trying to kill me, aren't you?"

"You are here to please me, wench." He thrust three fingers into her quim. "And it pleases me to taste you, to feel your body close to exploding with need."

"Sadistic bastard." She bit her lip when he looked up at her. "I'll do whatever you want. Just fuck me. Please, M'Lord."

She deserved another punishment for that comment. Still Kir couldn't ignore her pleas any longer. What she wanted was what he wanted more than anything at that moment. He needed to feel that connection with her. To be deep inside her.

He rose up so that his face was above hers, his hips pressed between her quivering thighs. "Take my cock in hand," he ordered.

Abby quickly reached between them and wrapped her small warm fingers around his length. Her cheeks glistened with tears of need and he bent to lick them from her face.

She tried to bring his cock to the opening of her channel but he shook his head. Despite the fact that he was near to bursting himself he said, "Stroke me."

She began moving her hand up and down his shaft, from balls to tip and back. "You're not going to come and leave me hanging, are you, M'Lord?"

He met her gaze. "As punishment perhaps I should continue to disallow your own pleasure. You seem to be unable to remember your place, wench."

Abby bit her lower lip and tightened her fingers around his cock as she worked it harder. "I am sorry, M'Lord."

"Release me." He pulled away from her hand, grasped his cock and brought it to her core. She pushed her hips up to meet him, but he teased her with the head of his erection, rubbing her drenched folds and making her shudder with the need to climax.

"Do you want me to fuck you, kitten?"

"Yes! Yes, M'Lord." She grasped his buttocks, digging her fingers into his muscled ass. "Fuck me, please!"

Kir drove his cock into Abby's quim.

She screamed loud enough to startle more *eloin* from the trees. "You feel so incredible."

Slowly he began to pump his staff in and out of her slick core. "So good. So tight. You grip me like an iron fist." His muscles corded as he worked to maintain control and to not spill his seed into her quim. Yet. "You were made for me."

Abby raked her nails from his ass to his back and he grew impossibly harder from the pain and pleasure of it.

"What do you say?" he demanded.

She dug her nails into his shoulders and thrust her hips up against his. "Yes. Yes! I was made for you, M'Lord."

"Only me," he growled.

"Only you, M'Lord."

Satisfaction filled him at her words. Their flesh was slick as he rocked against her. The smell of their sex rose up, surrounding them, blending with the scent of the ocean and the forest.

"Harder, faster," she begged. "Until I can feel you in my throat."

He fucked her harder then, no longer able to keep the slow pace. He drove into her so hard her thighs were surely bruised from his hips. The sound of flesh smacking flesh, their harsh breathing, the pounding of his heart, was louder in his ears than the constant roar of the ocean.

"I swear I'm going to die if I don't come." Abby had a glazed, feral look to her eyes. "You're killing me, M'Lord."

He ground his teeth. He couldn't let her command her own climax. He had to refrain a bit longer.

He fucked her harder. "Hold, wench."

Abby whimpered, tears flowing freely down her cheeks. No doubt a week of frustration and what he was putting them both through now was going to pay off in a way she would never expect.

He thrust two times, three times, four times more, then released his magical hold on her climax and shouted, "Come, kitten!"

Abby screamed louder than he had ever heard a woman scream. Her body shook and bucked and trembled and he swore he saw an aura form around her, could see the stars glittering in her mind.

"Oh, god," she kept shouting as her quim clenched and unclenched around his cock. "Ohgodohgodohgod!"

Kir couldn't take it any longer. He fucked her as hard as he could, drawing out her orgasm, then let loose with his own. His shout echoed through the forest, over his mountain, as his cock pulsed inside Abby's core.

Colored lights sparked in his head like he had never seen before. He swore the whole world turned upside down as he collapsed against her, barely keeping his whole weight off her. He rolled onto his side, taking Abby with him, his cock still throbbing in her quim. She continued to shiver and shake and moan.

When their breathing had slowed and the world righted itself, Kir knew he could never share this woman with another man.

He opened his eyes to meet Abby's.

"Wow," she said. "Let's do that again, M'Lord."

Chapter Thirteen

ॐ

Amazing didn't even come close to how Abby felt wrapped in Kir's arms. He held her so tightly, so securely, as if he truly planned to never let her go. His semi-hard cock still buried between her thighs only reinforced the sensation of belonging. There was something exciting yet frightening about the moment. She trembled with the mere thought of calling Emerald City her home—of calling this man her own.

What, was she crazy? She'd only known him for a week, yet already an ache formed in her heart at the thought of actually leaving him.

But she had to. She needed—wanted—her freedom, and she knew he would never give it to her.

Soft kiss after soft kiss he pressed to her neck, nuzzling her like he couldn't get enough of her. It was such an unfamiliar feeling and the moment felt somewhat awkward. Her body stiffened while his heart continued to pound against her chest. His breathing, light and warm, brushed her skin and raised tiny goose bumps across her flesh.

"Yes," he murmured and then nipped her throat. Startled, she squealed and he chuckled.

His tenderness stole her senses away, melted the tension. "What, M'Lord?" She couldn't think, didn't want to do anything but feel and smell the sweet chemistry their bodies made rubbing together as he began a slow rhythm moving in and out of her pussy.

"Yes, I will make love to you again, but," he stilled, rose upon the palms of hands and stared deep into her eyes, "each time you feel close to climax you must reveal something about yourself."

He ground his hips against hers and then smiled. Immediately he began to harden, growing firm and thick, filling her body.

Abby's eyes widened. "Me?" Did the man actually want to know more about her than she was a good lay? Had she ever met a man that was interested in knowing what made Dorothy Abigail Osborne tick, after sex?

Before the intimate act — yeah. That was part of the game.

"I want to know everything about you." He dipped his head and kissed her lips lightly.

Abby's pulse leaped. A taut feeling crowded her throat. She'd never been in a situation like this. Never knew, but always wondered, what it would be like to lay with a man and talk about her dreams, her aspirations...the future.

Okay, girl, you're getting ahead of yourself. He only asked for a few minor details like mom, dad, brothers, sisters. Not what you want out of life.

"I want to know what is in your heart." He lowered his weight upon her and began to rock gently.

He did something with his hips that drove him deeper and made her choke over her words. "My heart?"

"Mmmm... Your heart. Who are you? What do you wish out of life?"

Nobody. A home. Someone to love me. She barely held back her thoughts. "There's nothing special about me."

Again he rose on his palms. He frowned. Finally, he said, "Then you do not see what I do." He brushed an errant lock of hair from her face. "You are the most beautiful creature I have ever laid eyes on." Her pulse fluttered. "You're strong and determined and hardheaded." He playfully grinned, leaned forward and traced her lips with his tongue. "You taste good. And…" Kir pressed his length to hers, "…you are mine."

Mine. Moisture welled in her eyes. *Mine. Why do I wish that were true? One week, Abby. Only one week!*

He thrust deep and hard into her body. "Now feel, do not think. Lock your long, gorgeous legs around my waist."

The action widened her thighs and drew him closer. The result was a release of desire that made his ride slicker, faster, deeper. Her womb began to throb. A pulsation she knew he felt when he said, "Tell me now."

Breathlessly, she said, "My parents are deceased. My aunt and uncle raised me. I am an only child." The emotion behind her words chased the climax away. He held her tighter as if he sensed her loss and struggled to give comfort.

What type of man gave assuagement instead of seeking his own fulfillment?

Softly he whispered, "Kitten, I am so sorry," as his hand slipped between them and caressed her nipple. "I, too, am without parents or siblings." His confession was like a gravitational pull. She wrapped her arms around him and began to stroke his firm body, holding him and sensing a closeness that she had never felt with another human being.

Her chest rose, pressing her breast into the palm of his hand. The magic that his fingers performed—pinching, squeezing and pulling—yanked on those invisible ties to her pussy and again her sex tightened.

"Now," he muttered, his hips working in a slow burn. Fire licked the walls of her channel and she couldn't rationalize her thoughts.

"I'm lonely, frightened and scared." *Shit. Where did that come from?* The heat of embarrassment fanned her face. Her skin felt taut, like it had shrunk two sizes too small.

"Never again." She heard the promise in his strong voice. His determination stroked her body like a warm fire, chasing away her doubt and wrapping around her like a coat of security.

This is crazy. You don't know this man. Still she couldn't help feel that he meant every word.

Three more times he brought her close to climax and three more times she shared intimate details about her life, the farm and her dreams. Something in her took flight, as if her burdens sprouted wings and flew away, leaving her raw and vulnerable.

Then her channel clenched him like a sheath. She felt his cock pulse, jerk, as if he held on by a thread to his own orgasm. As the waves of release threatened to overcome her, she opened her mouth to reveal yet another secret, but this time he stole her words in a soul-searing kiss. He drank hungrily.

"Now, precious, come for me now."

She arched into his body, releasing a cry of ecstasy as every fiber of her body came alive. Nerves felt like fuses, his words a propellant lighting them so that they sizzled, bright and hot. She writhed beneath him, loving the way he pinned her to the earth, his strength, even his dominance. He was the ruler of this kingdom and quickly becoming the ruler of her heart.

* * * * *

Three weeks passed and Abby found herself becoming used to the sexual torture and pleasure Kir shared with her. After that first time, they had shared more secrets about one another and she felt herself growing closer and closer to him.

But when she asked about her freedom—that, he wouldn't listen to.

When she'd expressed her concern about becoming pregnant, he had explained how werewolves could control their seed so that his mate would become heavy with child only if both of them desired it.

To Abby's increasing surprise, she loved how Kir tied her up and spanked her, how he used all the toys in the dungeon to make her crazy with the need to climax. And then how he fucked her until she screamed with her amazing orgasms.

And somewhere in her heart, she found herself caring for him, like she had never cared for anyone before. It was in the way he looked at her. The way he talked with her. The mere fact that he wanted her as his packmate was exciting. No one had ever thought that way about her. Well, not that anyone could have wanted her to be his packmate. But it was the fact that he seemed to need her as much as he wanted her.

There was the respect given and received from his people. His strength. His tenderness. The way he held her, kissed her, as if she were the only woman alive. Hell, he didn't even look twice at Linara, or any of the other beautiful — not to mention naked — women in Emerald City.

But in her mind and soul, she rebelled against submitting to him anywhere but when they were alone. She wanted, needed, her freedom.

Today they were on the beach again and Abby was ready for another round of incredible sex. Kir was the best she had ever had. No way was she leaving this place without a few more performances.

Yet the thought of leaving Kir at all…somehow it tore her up inside.

Abby lounged on her back on the sand after being fucked out of her mind by Kir, and he was still between her thighs. Her arms rested behind her head while she listened to the sounds of waves lapping at the shore, so close she could imagine the waters flowing over her. The ground was feather-soft beneath her as she gazed into Kir's sapphire eyes. The intensity they held only moments ago had vanished, replaced by an expression of warmth she didn't understand. But she felt it, as if a ray of sunshine filtered through her naked body. A cool ocean breezed followed that warmth to stroke her flesh and bead her nipples.

In a slow, steady draw she pulled the masculine scent of his golden skin into her lungs and savored the heady fragrance. Through heavy lashes, she scanned up and down his muscular biceps that rested alongside her head. He bent and gently nibbled her earlobe. The tender action brought a sigh of contentment from her parted lips as her body arched, her taut buds scraping his chest.

Still wedged between her thighs, his rock-hard cock filled her, completed her. His hips pumped in and out of her slowly, her inner muscles clenching tightly around him. The thrust of his erection lulled her into a blissful state.

For the moment, Abby wanted nothing more than to lie in his arms and listen to his breathing joined by the melody of the ocean lapping at the shoreline.

She hadn't thought of home for hours and hours. That had to be a record. As the realization invaded her mind, a wave of disquiet shook her.

Abby couldn't help but worry about Aunt Maye and the farm and the need to make sure they were all okay.

And every single night for the past month Balin had continued to invade her dreams, calling to her, reminding her of home and of her freedom.

Freedom was what she wanted, yes?

Yet after only a month she'd found that Kir was everything she had dreamed of. A woman could spend a lifetime looking for her soulmate. Had she found hers in this strange and exotic universe? For a heartbeat Abby knew she held happiness within her hands and she knew that wonderful feeling would slip from her grasp when she left.

And if she chose freedom over Kir, she would have to deceive him and abandon him to return to her world. Her arms tightened around him. He continued to move slowly in and out of her body, unaware of the internal battle she fought.

Would leaving hurt him?

Can he feel real emotional pain?

Anger, yes, she'd seen that emotion. But would he miss her? Would his body and soul grieve for her as she knew she would grieve for him?

Her hips rose, taking him deeper, needing to take all of him inside her.

And what about his heart?

Little by little he was thawing toward the absolute domination thing, giving her a bit of pause—but not much. Somehow he knew she liked the challenge, as she knew he did. Instinctively he understood her needs, her desires. It was almost eerie, but thrilling at the same time, as if they were two halves of a whole.

He growled, grinding his hips against hers.

Suddenly she didn't know why it was so important to go home. What did she really have there anyway? Aunt Maye? The farm? If she wasn't there to till the fields, feed the animals, someone else would take her place. If only Abby knew her aunt was okay she might be able to adjust to this new world. Well...maybe.

Then an image of Balin, his hand outstretched, materialized in her mind. That one picture spoke so loud and she could still hear his voice telling her he would send her back to Kansas.

Where I'm from. To the freedom I should have. Abby bit back a sigh. She didn't belong here. Not really.

She couldn't live with Kir's arrogant domination forever—especially outside the bedroom.

The pit of her stomach felt hollow and a little cold.

She had to stay focused. She couldn't forget her submission was, at base, a game to keep Kir placated until Balin could rescue her.

Whenever the hell that might be.

Damn it.

Did all the men of this world take their fucking time with everything?

But since she was trapped indefinitely, why not enjoy what she had for the moment? Wasn't that what life was about? Taking happiness when and where you could find it? Even if was only temporary.

Kir banished the chill from her body when he cupped her face in his palms, thumbs stroking a path across her cheekbones. She loved the way he referred to her horrible freckles as faerie kisses. The way he slid his strong hands over the imperfections she had tried years to hide beneath makeup. Funny how this man made the flaws insignificant, even made her proud because they gave him such joy.

His touch was light, gentle, even cherishing, as his hand closed around her throat. He held a finger to her pulse, counting beats out loud, "One, two, three…" as they melted into the rhythm of his.

Then a wicked gleam flickered in his eyes. His gaze slid across her body, heating her blood. Kir looked at her as if she was the only woman in world. No man had ever made her feel so complete. Then he moved, easing out of her pussy and off her body.

Emptiness, a sense of loss, immediately consumed Abby. The desperate feeling was earthshaking, as if without him she wasn't whole. The thought was enough to have her second-guessing her sanity. *What the hell is going on with me?*

"Get on your hands and knees. I want to fuck you from behind." His hoarse voice revealed his desire, wiping away her insecurities.

Excitement sliced through Abby. Her nipples pebbled into aching points. Her pussy wept with anticipation. She was up for this and much, much more with this man.

Abby had barely settled on her hands and knees when the forest came alive. It began with a lone wolf's long, wailing cry, quickly answered by another from the north, the south, followed by the east and west.

A sudden movement in the forest startled a flock of *eloin* birds. As the birds streaked against the turquoise sky, she heard the swish of wings flapping, high-pitch shrills renting the air, and saw the flash of blue and magenta feathers.

A variety of animals — Abby thought she recognized a squirrel, a muskrat and a ferret — scampered from the bushes. Another, an animal like a rabbit experiment gone wrong — with the mixed breeding of a hamster and a fox — fled in the other direction.

Damn if it didn't sound like a whole freaky zoo had been let loose in the woods surrounding them.

A hiss like escaping stream sounded, chased by a choir of deep menacing growls. A series of loud roars countered, sending Abby scrabbling to get to her feet, and her heart to pounding like mad. At home she could deal with a stubborn horse or cow, but the sounds shaking the treetops were cats, big cats.

Kir's firm grip on Abby's hips held her in place. His thighs tight against her ass, his erection pressed between her parted legs, easing along her hot, wet slit. And then he thrust into her, causing her to cry out at the bliss of it.

But she knew something was coming.

"Kir, let me up," Abby panted as she wrenched her neck and looked over her shoulder at him. When he refused to release her, she tried to pin him with an aggravated glare, but failed when he thrust harder and forced a moan from her lips.

"Silence." He countered her glare with a withering stare, then cocked his head and listened, stroking her breast, one and then the other. She leaned into his palms as she watched him over her shoulder, while he continued to fuck her. His features were intense until a lone wolf-call answered the fierce cries.

Kir tweaked Abby's nipple and she yipped. "We have guests," he said, but he didn't stop driving into her. Instead his strokes intensified. The thought that the "guests" might soon see them both scared and excited her.

Oh, god, her climax was building and building. He was driving her closer to the edge of sanity. She cared about being seen, yet didn't give a damn at the same time. She moaned and he pinched her nipples harder and she cried out.

"May I come, M'Lord?" she begged, needing release and wanting it before whomever it was arrived.

"No."

Abby almost cried. She kept looking out for anyone who might be coming while Kir kept on fucking her. Just when she thought she'd seriously lose her mind, Kir shouted, "Come, kitten!" and she shrieked with a soul-deep orgasm that rocked her so hard she saw stars. Her arms gave out and her face would have been buried in the sand if it wasn't for Kir holding her up while he drove in and out of her.

In the next moment he howled, and she felt the power of his orgasm and his warm come jetting inside her.

While she was still trying to catch her breath, he rose and extended his hand. She frowned but accepted his assistance, her legs still shaking and her pussy still spasming as she got to her feet.

Abby bent and brushed off her knees, rubbing sand from her palms. A stinging slap to her ass had her spinning to face Kir.

She raised one brow.

He smiled, leaning over to kiss her softly. She melted at his touch, wanting nothing more than to get closer. Instead he took a step backward.

"The King of Spades and the King of Clubs are nearing. I must welcome them to Emerald City." He stretched his arms wide, his tan skin absorbing the morning's rays. In quick movements he shook his mane, his hair floating on the light breeze, feathering across his shoulders. Abby had never seen a man so in tune with the world around him. So gorgeous.

And just like that, the man before her shapeshifted into a golden wolf. Waves and waves of lustrous fur covered his body. His sapphire eyes were the only thing recognizable of the man who had once stood before her.

Abby shook her head. Only moments ago he had been in his human form. Now here he stood on four legs with an ominous air of danger surrounding him. Still she wanted to touch him. Run her hands through all that soft fur.

As Abby reached for him, Kir growled and playfully nipped at her hand. She swatted at his muzzle but he leaped out of her reach. In either form, Kir was breathtaking.

You must mind your manners when our guests are present, he spoke to her telepathically, as Balin had done again last night. *I am proud of you, kitten. I want my friends to see my treasure.* Kir turned and began to lope toward the forest.

Was that all she was to Lord Kir, a possession? The indignation of it all made Abby's blood boil. Her temper ignited like a stick of dynamite. It sizzled up her spine, stiffening her shoulders.

"If I can't dazzle them with my brilliance, *M'Lord*, I'll baffle them with bullshit," she called out, her tone heavy with sarcasm.

He stopped in his tracks. Slowly, he swung his head in her direction. His eyes glowed with the heat of his words. *Heed me well, my wild one. If you embarrass me, you will be punished.*

Duh. As if she hadn't expected that threat to follow his oh-so-anticipated warning.

He bared his teeth and snarled.

She pulled back her lips, displaying her pearly whites, and hissed right back at him.

A shake of his head said it all. Still Abby thought she saw him smile. Could wolves smile? The man simply didn't know what to do with her and she loved it. Actually she got the greatest kick out of sparring with him. It was a sensual act of foreplay that made her horny as hell.

With another growl, he pivoted and trotted off to meet his guests.

Abby released a frustrated breath as her fists dug into her hips. "Well, hell." She watched Lord Kir in wolf-form disappeared around the side of the mountain. "We were getting on so well."

Just under the cover of trees at the edge of the forest, she could see a ménage à trois—a man and two women engaged in hot and heavy sex. Their soft moans floated on the breeze and made her ache to be in Kir's arms again. A little way down the beach, another couple stroked and caressed each other. Where the hell did they all come from? Not long ago it had been just her and Lord Kir on the beach. Had these other people watched her and Kir fucking? That thought sent heat straight to her cheeks.

Where was O? The damn animal had disappeared again. He had really taken to the beach and the surrounding forest.

This is such a strange world. Abby turned and gazed out longingly over the waves, thinking of Kir. His touch, the way he looked at her with those incredible eyes—like she was the only woman in the world for him.

"Why couldn't I have met you in Kansas or Kentucky, even Texas?" Hell, Tennessee for that matter. She loved the way he pronounced Kansas, as Kanzaz. Her chest squeezed tight. Crap. Why on Earth had she let this man slip into her heart?

"I can't stay here. I won't." As Abby gathered her resolve, she heard female laughter approaching from behind her. In her mind she heard Kir's sensual voice.

The green-eyed monster slithered across Abby's skin. "Kings? He meant queens." She readied herself to give Kir a piece of her mind. What? He'd fuck her then bring forth other women because she wasn't enough?

When Abby whirled around, she froze stiff. A pack of wolves followed behind a pride of tigers.

That's right. Big, mean-looking tigers. With teeth, a mouthful. Long sharp claws that clicked as they met the small stones on the ground. Tawny coats striped with black, except for two of them, who were snowy-white with black stripes and larger than the rest.

Between them were two women riding horses unlike any Abby had ever seen. The animals' hides had the radiant glow of quicksilver. Their muzzles narrow, their bodies sleek, almost fragile looking. If you added a mother-of-pearl horn in the middle of their heads, she would have sworn they were from the mystical unicorn family. In fact, they were more beautiful and more graceful than any horse she had ever seen in Kansas.

Wedged between the women's horses was that dirty cur-dog, Kir. He rubbed gently on the redhead's leg, and then the leg of the woman with dark brown hair. His caresses elicited soft sighs from each woman's full lips.

Fear overrode fury when the two very large and dangerous white tigers broke from the group and headed straight for her. The rest of the pride and Kir's pack remained out of hearing distance but close enough for discomfort. Abby took several unsteady steps backward. Her pulse leaped. Unsure of whether she should run or plunge into the ocean, she backpedaled toward the water's edge.

A streak of white moved past her so quickly her stomach rolled, as did the ground beneath her. When her vision steadied, one tiger stood behind her, the other dead center. Terror rumbled through her veins, gooseflesh skittered across her skin.

"Nice kitties…" she said to the cats before she screamed, "Kir!"

Should she run or play dead? Didn't she hear somewhere that if you played dead a wild animal would just leave you alone? Apparently they loved the chase and they liked to tease their captives.

Funny how that sounded a lot like men.

They will not hurt you, Abby, they only seek to get to know you. Kir's voice attempted to reassure her. Unsuccessfully.

The cats moved with feline grace…closer…closer… Too close.

"Well, I don't care to become acquainted with anything with claws and teeth that sharp." Abby clenched her fists. "Call the sons of bitches off me."

The tiger behind her nudged her ass gently with his head. Fear and anger overrode common sense. "Back off, Jack." She reached around, swatting thin air.

His growl as he sidestepped her hand almost sounded like laughter.

Well, shit. That's all she needed. Animals laughing at her when she was scared shitless.

"Kir," she yelled again, just as the tiger once again poked her ass, causing her to stumble forward so that the cat in front of her buried his cold, wet nose in her crotch.

It was pure reflex. Abby's balled fist came down hard on the cat's right eye, as she hopped on one leg, trying to be rid of the cat's invasion.

The offended tiger roared, taking a couple steps back while shaking his head. His big blue eyes blinked several times as they began to water.

The look on Kir's face as he shifted into human form, not to mention the heavy steps bringing him to Abby's side, told her he was mad, steaming mad. His fingers closed brutally on her arm.

"You have earned a punishment," he growled low, shaking her. "Far worse than any you have received thus far."

She ground her teeth. "Fuck you."

Abby found herself on her knees faster than she could take a breath.

"You have insulted my guests." His hand landed none too gently on her shoulder as she tried to rise.

She glared up at Kir. "Your guests should learn manners and keep their noses to themselves."

"You are mine to do as I wish. That includes sharing you."

"Bullshit." The heat of anger scorched up Abby's face. Damn the man. Was she supposed to let the tigers fondle her? An image of their rough tongues lapping at her pussy brushed her mind.

Holy crap. She was losing it.

A breath caught in Abby's throat as the two tigers began to shapeshift. All that beautiful white fur twisted and churned. In moments, two scrumptious pieces of beefcake stood before her. Men so exquisite they would indeed have made a perfect addition to one of her nightly wet dreams — before she met Kir.

A man with white-blond hair, one gold earring and a large club tattoo in the center of his impressive six-pack frowned at her. His eye was turning red and it had begun to swell.

Shitshitshit. She was in trouble. *Big* trouble if Kir's red face was a meter gauging his anger.

The other cat-man had a dangerous air about him. A spade tattoo graced his left wrist and wild pecan-colored hair flowed past his shoulders, giving him that bad-boy look. His tiger earring only added to his mystery. He turned to the brown-haired female and together they broke into laughter.

Then bad boy held out his arms and the redheaded woman slipped off the horse and into his embrace. "It appears, my friend, that you have found trouble in the form of a little spitfire. A shame that we bring news of more."

Kir's fiery glare rose from Abby. He pivoted sharply to address spade-man. "Trouble?"

"Awai," club-man murmured, as he moved to the remaining woman on horseback. As if she was a piece of glass, he assisted her off her mount. When the man tenderly placed his palm on her rounded belly, Abby realized that his mate was pregnant.

The exquisite woman was dressed in a white, transparent robe trimmed in black lace that whispered across her protruding stomach. A black collar with club-shaped diamonds graced her slender neck. Shallow breaths pushed her full breasts against the silky material and her nipples were clearly visible. Her outfit was only held together by two golden clubs placed on each side of her waist. Her legs, as well as the gentle swell of her breasts and the dark patch between her thighs, were bare for all to see.

But who was Abby to talk, standing stark naked among the crowd? She felt a flush of embarrassment heat her body. The redhead made Abby long for her own clothing. The woman wore tight-fitting black leather breeches and a leather halter-top that revealed only enough to entice. And at the way spade-man was plucking at the strings of her shirt, she wouldn't be wearing it long, especially if he had anything to say.

The woman that club-man referred to as Awai drew her hand toward his injured face and caressed the now bruising flesh. His soft blue eyes looked down at her adoringly.

"Does it hurt, Ty?" she whispered.

"Yes." His boyish expression almost made Abby laugh.

"Good." Awai smacked him on the shoulder. "The woman is right. Your manners—and Darronn's—could be improved. Step aside," she pushed past the stunned man, "and let me meet the woman from my world."

She reached her hand out to Abby, who was still kneeling. When Abby made to rise, Kir growled softly. She gripped the woman's hand without standing.

Awai shook her head. "Welcome to Lord Kir's realm. The recipient of your right hook is my husband, Ty, the King of Clubs. I'm Awai. The burly beast next to my niece, Alexi, is

142

Darronn, the King of Spades. Alexi and I are so happy to meet someone from home."

The woman held herself regally, but her smile was warm and welcoming. Still Abby was on guard. Things in this world were not what they appeared to be. Balin had warned her of friends in wolves' clothing. Or fur in this case.

Abby wanted to shake off Kir's hold, but she forced herself to remain still as she looked up at Awai. "I'm Abby," she finally said.

Awai released her hand. "Well, Abby, I hope Lord Kir has been treating you well."

Before Abby could answer, Kir growled, "She must be punished immediately. She has offended the King of Clubs."

"Later." Alexi moved towards them. "We want to talk. Besides, Darronn caused this incident purposely, if I know my man. Abby wasn't to blame."

"Still, she will be punished," Kir insisted.

"Yeah, yeah." Alexi brushed her hand through the air several times. "Shoo. You guys will only be in the way. Besides, John Steele is loose and the bastard needs to be found before he can cause any further trouble."

"It is true," Ty answered Kir's questioning expression. "He slipped his chains two nights ago. We tracked him to the borders of Emerald City and Malachad." He glanced protectively towards Awai. "Awai is close to delivering our cubs. She will not rest knowing the man roams our lands."

Kir stepped away from Abby, moving toward his friend as he placed a comforting hand on Ty's shoulder. "She will be safe in Emerald City." He tilted his head skyward and released a beautiful howl. Immediately the pack of wolves that had escorted Kir and his friends moved forward. The pack surrounded them, each taking a protective position.

"Thank you, my comrade." Ty's gaze firmed as he looked at Awai then Alexi. "The women would not remain behind knowing that a kinswoman had come to our world."

Kir's brows pulled together. "How did you discover Abby's arrival?"

"The Munchfolk," Ty replied. "The disturbing winds brought them out in droves. They saw you rescue Abby from her car." A smirk crossed his face. "In fact, they said—"

Awai cleared her throat. "Ty." It was a soft warning.

Ty moved from Kir to gather Awai in his arms. He nuzzled her neck. The love he showed for this woman warmed Abby's heart. Could anyone ever love her like that?

Could Kir?

At the same time, Kir moved to Abby's side and assisted her to her feet. "Car?" he asked.

Damned if her knees didn't ache from that short period of kneeling. Kir moved behind her and his warm palms cupped the nape of her neck. Gently he began to massage. His naked body pressed against hers. Still pissed, she attempted to move away, but his arms snaked around her waist. His cock burned into her back. Memories of their tender loving softened her stance and she leaned back into him.

"It is a machine, a mode of transportation, from what Alexi tells me," Darronn said. "I am told the stench was overpowering." He caressed the horse standing beside him. "Thank you, Tok of the *jul*, and your mate, Lorali, for escorting our women to Emerald City."

Amazingly the horse spoke. "It is an honor to carry your queens." The animal stretched one leg out before him and bowed gracefully.

Abby's eyes bulged. "Did that friggin horse...er, animal just talk?"

Alexi and Awai laughed.

"Yes. The *jul* are close friends with the Kings of Tarok and Lord Kir," responded Alexi. "Freaky, isn't it?"

Kir's palm caressed Abby's stomach as he looked at Awai's extended belly, giving Abby the heebie-jeebies. She stared down at Kir's hand, to Awai's abdomen, then back at the hand upon her.

"Don't even think about it."

"Kir, a daddy?" Awai laughed. "Can't see it. He's the ladies man of all the land. There would be too many broken hearts. Mine included."

Abby didn't like the sound in the woman's voice, nor the way her gaze stroked Kir.

Ty growled softly against Awai's ear.

Abby looked over her shoulder to see Kir with the corner of his mouth quirked into a smile.

"Ty and Kir share everything," explained Awai, her almond-shaped eyes glowing with a wicked glint.

Abby's jaw dropped.

"Believe me, you'll enjoy every minute of it." Awai's words gave Abby the same result as being tossed around by a tornado. Shock and disbelief only touched the fringes of what was running through her mind. Her gazed darted to Alexi. The gleam in the woman's eyes burned as hot as Awai's and the three men staring at her.

Oh shit! Dorothy Abigail Osborne was in trouble...deep, deep trouble.

Chapter Fourteen

🔊

With both amusement and jealousy, Kir watched the play of emotion that danced across Abby's features. She looked intrigued and frightened all at once at the suggestion of being taken by these men and women.

Kir's own jealousy surprised him. He had often shared women with Darronn and Ty and had always found it most enjoyable. However, that was before the two kings had found their lifemates.

And the thought of either one of them taking Abby made Kir want to growl and bare his teeth. She was *his*.

"Um, yeah," Abby finally said after Awai's sensual statement. Abby attempted to move away, but Kir kept her trapped tight against his length. Just the feel of her body against his made him want to fuck her right there, in front of everyone. And he had the feeling she would most definitely enjoy it. "Sounds fun, but," she jerked her thumb toward the forest, "I think I'll just wait over there."

Darronn wrapped his arm protectively around the shoulders of his wife and queen, Alexi. "I have never," he looked pointedly at Kir, "and would never share my woman with any man."

Alexi elbowed him and slipped out of his dominating embrace. "I'm sure Abby knows we were just teasing her."

Awai gave a soft laugh and winked at Abby. "This is a world of many delights, and there is only pleasure in sharing partners and absolutely no shame in doing so. Ty and I simply will have no one but each other."

Kir remembered the moment when he and Rafe were supposed to share Awai with Ty, but Kir had sensed the two only wanted one another—it had just taken them each awhile to recognize it.

Kir held on tighter to Abby. He knew he had found his own packmate in this spitfire of a kitten. Like the kings and their queens, Kir now could not begin to imagine sharing Abby with any man *or* woman.

Abby relaxed against him, her naked body warm next to his. "I'm all for pleasure," she said, her voice filled with bravado that lacked conviction. She shrugged. "Bring it on."

It was Kir who growled this time and Abby glanced up at him with surprise, and perhaps a bit of fear in her expression. Good. She feared him. As it should be—he was lord of this realm and all bowed to him. She should have no doubt that she was *his*.

The—ah—bowing to him and accepting his lordship part—that might take a while longer...

"Why don't you go do your macho man-thing, while we get a chance to get acquainted with Abby?" Alexi shooed them away with a wave of her hands.

Instead of being annoyed by the woman's lack of submissive protocol, Kir found himself amused. But then his thoughts returned to their revelation that John Steele had escaped from his prison in Tarok. Steele, the man who had once beaten Awai when she was married to him in the otherworld. Steele had been brought to Tarok to be taught a lesson, but now it seemed that lesson hadn't been enough.

Kir gave a nod to each of his comrades, Darronn, then Ty. "We have much to discuss."

Ty and Darronn kissed their women, then shifted into white tigers. Kir sensed Abby's amazement and she jumped aside when he released her to transform into a wolf.

Behave, he warned her through mind-thought. *You have already earned a tremendous punishment.*

Abby just glared at him and folded her arms beneath her breasts, causing them to rise and her nipples to jut out in a most enticing manner. His keen werewolf senses drank in the scent of their earlier lovemaking and he wished only to shift back into a man, take her to his room and fuck her again and again until she agreed to give him her body, heart and soul.

The sudden thought that he wanted her heart and soul nearly made him stagger.

He shook it off, turned and loped toward Emerald City, the tigers at his sides.

When they reached the war room, Ty, Darronn and Kir shifted into men. Each man was dressed in leather breeches and stood around the three-dimensional map that encompassed Oz, as well as the Kingdoms of Tarok and the Kingdom of Malachad.

Kir folded his arms across his chest and faced his two friends. "This John Steele—you have tracked him this far?"

Darronn gave a single nod. He pointed to the land that bordered the lush forest of Emerald City. "We lost his scent on the outskirts of your realm when the stench of *bakir* overwhelmed Steele's. Perhaps the bastards took Steele to Balin."

With a low growl Kir said, "We have *bakir* prisoners. We will interrogate them further to see if they can tell us of this man." Kir lowered his arms and clenched his fists. "So far my warriors have been unable to break their silence."

"Beasts." Ty's voice was nearly a roar. "Let *me* at them. I will not have them harm my queen or the cubs she carries in her womb. If the *bakirs* will not speak then we will set out to track Steele at once."

Kir placed his palm on Ty's shoulder. "Patience, my friend. We may now face two enemies. If by chance Steele and Balin have combined efforts we must ensure we do not walk into a trap."

"More likely Balin has killed Steele for stumbling into his realm," offered Darronn as he watched concern filter across his brother's anxious features.

Ty's muscles tightened beneath Kir's grip. The King of Clubs stepped away. A vein twitched in his jaw, his glare burning into the map. "I cannot rely on that possibility, nor will Awai. We must know what has befallen Steele. The man is a danger to Awai's well-being and that of our cubs." Almost as if it were issued as a promise, Ty murmured, "I will not let him near my family."

The air in the room thickened as Darronn and Kir exchanged glances. Kir sensed there was more, something sinister lingering. Never had he detected vulnerability in the two kings, but at that moment it was there in their strained stance, the creases in their foreheads.

"The man is but a human. What really threatens you?" Kir's question stirred both kings as they shifted their gazes to his.

"Balin." Darronn clenched his fists until they paled. Hatred flickered, sparking a red flame in the depths of the King of Spades' eyes. "The demon feeds on weakness, a person's doubts and fears. We worry our queens' insecurities will open a path to his mind control. He has been quiet too long, as if he silently waits for a door to open, an opportunity to prevail."

The war room door burst open and Janan entered. Heavy footsteps rang across the stone floor. His dusky hair was wild. His blue eyes were colder than an iceberg. His face was flushed red. "They're dead. All of them—dead."

149

The fine hairs on Kir's nape sprang to life. For a moment Abby's face flashed before his vision. Her beautiful smile. The littering of faerie kisses across her nose and cheeks. Fear like he had never experienced twisted through his veins. His gut clenched.

He sensed Ty and Darronn tensing beside him.

"Who?" Kir's voice was tight, brittle as if the single word broke rather than flowed from his mouth.

Janan's fingers threaded through his long mane. His head was bowed as if he couldn't face his master's displeasure. "The *bakirs*."

Kir released the breath he'd been holding. Darronn and Ty followed suit. The women were safe.

Kir took a step toward his captain. "Janan, what happened?"

Janan shook his head disbelievingly. "Massacre. It's as if they tore one another apart. Blood... Flesh shredded..." The man's voice faltered. Failure was written across his features.

Uneasiness stirred in Kir's belly. "The *bakirs* were imprisoned, chained separately. How could their deaths be possible?"

"Their restraints were removed. Locks picked clean." Janan shook his head. "The guard outside the cells never moved from his post. He heard no sounds."

"Then how?" barked Darronn.

Janan dropped to one knee. He lifted his face to Kir. "Either we have a traitor amongst us, or the walls of Emerald City have been breached."

Fury whirled throughout Kir's body. His sanctuary had been penetrated. He had offered safety to his friends and their queens only to discover it was a farce.

"Increase the guards on the perimeter," Kir growled his command. Janan rose, pivoted sharply and without a word marched through the open door. Kir's movements were slow with a dangerous air of menace as he turned toward Darronn and Ty. "It's time to put an end to this battle. We leave within the hour."

Ty looked from Darronn to Kir. "What about the women?"

"My sanctuary has been breached." Kir slammed his fist on the map table. "I fear they will not be safe without our protection."

Darronn crossed his arms. "Then they must come with us."

* * * * *

"I'm not going anywhere with you." Abby planted her hands on her hips. "Just send me back home. I don't belong in this nutty place and you have no business keeping me prisoner."

"Quiet, wench!" Kir bellowed but Abby didn't even flinch. O, on the other hand, wagged his tail, eager to begin the journey.

Still maintaining her stiff posture and defiant stare, she took a step forward. "Make me."

From behind him Kir heard Awai's snicker and Alexi's outright laugh. The two kings merely kept their arms folded across their chests and gave their mates a you're-next-in-line-for-a-punishment stare.

Neither seemed to care at all.

Kir's skin heated and a flush of anger traveled from head to toe. How dare she speak to him that way before the entire hunting party? "You *will* obey."

Abby opened her mouth, but before she spewed forth another retort, Kir swept her up and slung her onto the *jul* so that she hung over the creature on her belly.

"Oof." The very unladylike grunt squeezed from between her thin lips. "Let me down!" she shouted and then cried out when Kir swatted her naked ass with his bare hand. Her cry turned into a moan of desire when he swatted her again and he caught the musky scent of her juices.

With a feeling of extreme satisfaction, he swung up on the beast so that he was seated on the *jul's* bare back, and drew Abby onto his leather-clad lap. She kicked and struggled, but he simply spanked her, once then twice more. He sensed her oncoming orgasm and used his powers to keep her from coming. She would be punished for her impudence and for punching the King of Clubs, and she would not be allowed to climax until she behaved and saw to his every pleasure.

After they were safe.

Rather than shifting into his wolf form like his warriors, Kir had chosen to ride with the kings and their queens in order to keep Abby close to him. He didn't trust her not to attempt escape in his absence. But more than that, he felt the incredible urge to have her near him at all times. When he was away from her, he could do naught but think about her lovely body, her fiery spirit, the way she felt whenever he buried his cock deep inside her quim.

Was this the vulnerability he had sensed in the kings earlier? Did the need for a woman transform a man into a weak shell of his former self?

But no. He sensed the kings were as strong as they ever had been. Yet that sense of protectiveness, that concern, could make a man drop to his knees.

Although everyone in their hunting party was dressed in leathers, including Kir himself, he'd forced Abby to remain naked. It pleased him to see her beautiful body and it pleased him to know that the other men in the party, especially Prince Eral, wanted her, but knew she belonged to him.

At the same time it maddened Kir, a feeling of protectiveness and jealousy that threatened to overwhelm him.

Regardless of whether or not she would admit it, Abby wanted him, and she wanted him now. He had no doubt he could take her in front of every member of the hunting party and she would beg him for more.

"You son of a bitch," Abby was saying, along with a stream of words that no one should say to the lord of any realm. Kir simply withdrew a scarf from the saddlebag and slipped it between Abby's lips in mid-rant and tied it snugly behind her head. Only a gurgling sound of anger issued from her now, and she tried to reach up and pull the gag from her mouth. In a few quick movements, Kir had another scarf tied around her wrists so that her arms were bound behind her back. Now she couldn't fight him and she had to keep her damned mouth shut.

O barked. If a dog could frown, he was frowning at Kir's treatment of his mistress. "She is well, my friend. Just needs a strong hand," Kir assured the animal.

Abby slumped over his lap, apparently giving in to her position. He had no doubt she would be fighting mad when he finally released her and it surprised him to realize he was looking forward to it.

While the hunting party set out to find Steele, Kir growled beneath his breath as he thought about the deaths of the *bakirs*. What filth had penetrated his sanctuary to perform such a despicable act?

He would find the vermin and ensure they paid for their deeds.

There was comfort in knowing his fellow comrades were beside him—Ty and Darronn, as well as Prince Eral, would always watch his back and fight alongside him.

Kir's realm extended far from Emerald City. The *juls'* hooves barely made a sound as they stepped through the pine needles and leaves, fallen branches and twigs littering the forest floor. Kir drank deep of the scents of trees, rich loam and the smells of the forest's wildlife. His senses were keenly aware of all that moved around him. A rabbit scurrying for cover beneath a bush, a fox slipping into its den, a fawn trembling next to a doe. But a man—only a faint odor tinted the air. An odor that must be days old.

While they rode—despite the ache in his cock with Abby on his lap—Kir and his companions enjoyed light conversation. But the purpose of their ride was in every man's eyes, as it was in Alexi's and Awai's. Kir's scouts loped ahead, ensuring the way was clear and free of Balin's traps, should the Sorcerer have entered his realm. Kir growled at the mere thought.

If he got his hands on Balin, Kir would strangle the bastard for all that he had done to Mikaela as well as the kings and queens of Tarok. Now the King of Malachad was invading Kir's territory, and it was even more personal.

By the time the hunting party stopped for the evening, Kir wanted to fuck Abby so badly he could have taken her ten times over. But instead he swung down from his mount and scooped Abby up in his arms. When she was on her feet, standing before him, her cinnamon eyes were blazing, her head tilted up defiantly at him. O appeared to have the same expression plastered on his furry muzzle.

Even though he wanted absurdly to smile, Kir kept his features and his voice stern. "Lower your gaze, wench, or you shall not be released from any of your bonds."

For a moment she refused to avoid eye contact with him, but she finally dropped her gaze.

Prince Eral approached. His smile was too broad, the desire in his eyes too bright. He bowed. "Do you require my services, M'Lord?"

Kir growled.

The Prince's grin grew. "Of course, I offer to take the animal, perhaps feed him?" His appreciative gazed scanned Abby from head to toe.

Jealousy was an unfamiliar feeling and Kir did not like it. "Thank you, Prince Eral."

Eral bowed again then reached for O's collar. "As always, it is my pleasure." He began to drag the resisting dog away.

When prince and dog disappeared, Kir turned his attention back to Abby. "Widen your stance," he commanded. "Let me see your lovely quim."

Abby trembled with what he was certain was fury, but obeyed.

Around them the warriors were setting up camp, including a tent for Lord Kir and Abby, as well as a tent each for the kings and their mates.

He reached out and tweaked both her nipples with his fingers then pinched them hard. Abby gave a moan behind her gag and her features softened as she leaned into his touch. Just as he thought, she wanted him badly.

How it would please—and torture—him to make her wait.

"If you promise to remain quiet and to not attempt to run away I will release your bonds and your gag. Will you cooperate, wench?"

Abby hesitated for just the slightest of moments then gave a nod. With satisfaction Kir moved behind her and untied her wrists. Before releasing her, he massaged her arms. Then he turned her around but she kept her gaze lowered. He reached behind her head and untied the scarf and dropped it to the forest floor. Abby gave a shuddering sigh of relief. He captured her chin in his hand and forced her to gaze up at him. Primal instinct took over and he crushed his mouth to hers, delving deep into her warmth. Gods, how that sweet mouth would feel upon his cock right now.

In frustration he pushed her away. She looked up at him, a dazed expression on her face and lust in her eyes. "Join the women beside the fire," he commanded. "Sit cross-legged, your thighs splayed wide, so that all might see the treasure that is mine. And only mine."

Abby's eyes flared and as she turned away from him he almost laughed when she muttered under her breath, "Son of a bitch."

Why the woman's stubbornness and fiery nature appealed to him so, he did not understand. But it made the ache in his loins grow and his desire for her almost too much to bear.

She joined Awai and Alexi at the campfire. Both women were chatting and soon drew Abby into their conversation. Every now and then he would catch Abby's glare but she sat as he had ordered her to, cross-legged on a blanket before the fire. Just the sight of her soft curls, moist folds, and engorged clit made him bite back a groan. To see other men stare at her with lust in their eyes made him want to growl and stake his territory right there for all to see.

Kir had the feeling that Abby knew she was torturing him with his own form of punishment and was enjoying it too much as she spread her legs wider. His gaze darted towards Prince Eral, and as Kir expected, the man's eyes were pinned on Abby. As he scanned the party, Kir noted that the prince wasn't the only one enjoying the view.

After dinner he could take no more. Kir took Abby by her hair and drew her up from her sitting position. She cried out in surprise, but he knew she enjoyed the initial pain when he tugged at her hair, and that it gave her pleasure.

"Go inside and prepare for me, wench," he growled, pointing to his tent. "I want you on your knees, your thighs wide, your hands behind your back, your chest thrust forward and your gaze lowered. Do you understand?"

She glared at him but immediately dropped her gaze. "Yes, M'Lord," she replied through gritted teeth before she turned and marched to the tent. O jumped up from his place next to Prince Eral and made to follow Abby.

"Leave the dog outside," demanded Kir.

Just before Abby went inside she muttered something to O. The dog slid to his belly, lying next to the tent's opening. Abby shot a fresh glare in Kir's direction, extended her middle finger, and then she was gone.

Alexi laughed. "She just gave you the finger."

"Finger?" Kir asked, puzzled even though it was the third time she had done so.

Awai shared a knowing look with her niece before looking back to Kir. "It means 'fuck you'."

Kir straightened his shoulders. "I take it this is not a proper way for her to address the lord of this realm?"

Alexi rolled her eyes. "You really are in for it with her, Kir. Abby's not going to come around easily. She may not ever submit the way you want her to. It isn't natural for her."

With a soft laugh Awai added, "You'll be lucky if you can come to any sort of compromise with her. I'll bet she'll fight you all the way."

"Compromise." Kir snorted. "There will be no compromise. She is mine and will do as I dictate."

This time Alexi stifled a giggle. "We'll just see about that."

With a growl, Kir strode toward the tent, twigs and pine needles crunching beneath his boots. He flung open the tent flap and to his immense pleasure Abby was positioned as he had ordered.

He had a need that had to be fulfilled immediately, so that he might proceed with Abby's punishment.

"Look at me, wench." He unlaced his breeches and pulled out his very erect cock. Abby's eyes widened and she flicked her tongue along her lower lip. When he reached her, Kir grabbed her by her hair and tilted her face so that her mouth was even with his erection. "Do you want my cock?"

Abby licked her lips again. "Whatever pleases you, M'Lord."

Kir felt a moment of suspicion. She was giving in far too easily. But his need for her was so great that he shoved the thought aside and plunged his cock between her parted lips.

She started to bring her hands up. "Remain in position," he ordered as his grip tightened in her hair and he began to fuck her mouth. "Watch me."

Her eyes were wide as she took his length to the back of her throat. She flicked her tongue along his cock while he kept his grip on her hair and continued plunging in and out of her mouth. "Gods. Your mouth. So hot. So wet."

Kir's climax approached like an oncoming storm. Throughout the day the woman had tortured him out of his mind with her body, her struggles, her spirit. He would fill her mouth with his seed and then he would punish her.

Closer and closer he came to the pinnacle as he watched his cock move in and out of her mouth, saw her take him, accept him and enhance his pleasure with her tongue. With a roar he tilted back his head and spewed his fluid into Abby's mouth. Lights flashed behind his eyes and his body trembled with the force of his orgasm.

When he collected himself enough to look back at Abby, she was licking his cream from her lips, her eyes smoky with desire.

His cock hardened again. "On your hands and knees, facing the bed." When she obeyed, her backside to him, he saw the slickness of her thighs, her juices from her arousal. He rubbed his palm over each ass cheek and she trembled beneath his touch. "Do you want me to fuck you, kitten?"

"Yes, God, yes." Abby stilled. "I mean, if it pleases you, M'Lord."

"You must be punished for punching the king this morning." He lowered his voice to a near growl. "Not only that, you defied me, Abby. For all to see, you acted unbecoming."

"Yes, M'Lord," she said too easily. "I will take whatever punishment you think is necessary."

By the Gods, she wanted it. He knew she received great pleasure from her punishments.

Kir smiled to himself. The one thing he knew she didn't want was to wait for her orgasm…and that was exactly what he was going to make her do.

Wait.

Chapter Fifteen

ഇ

Kir moved in front of Abby, a majestic display of masculinity. She remained on her hands and knees, taking in the amazing sight. His engorged cock thrust high and straight from the blond nest of hair at his groin. The head of his erection was a deep purple hue, and it vibrated with the force of pounding blood.

He wanted her.

Abby smiled. Her tongue slid across her bottom lip as she inhaled the last of his lingering essence. The man had teased and taunted her the entire day with what the night might hold. Surely he couldn't know her need was so great that she'd say or do anything right now to feel his staff buried deep within her aching core.

Kir moved behind her and another shiver of delight skittered along her spine. Like a cat she stretched, dipping her back and lifting her ass for Kir's hot gaze. The need to climax burned throughout her body. Damn if she didn't feel like purring, rubbing her heated flesh back and forth across his, curling her body around him.

Something cold and wet nudged her anus and a sliver of fear sliced through her. No man had ever entered her there and what was even more frightening, by the temperature and the rock-hard touch, it wasn't Kir's penis. Before she could move or pull away, the object slid home, forcing a tight, high-pitched scream from her mouth. She lunged forward, scrambling on her hands and knees.

Strong, powerful hands grasped her waist and held her in place. "Be still, Abby. You have brought this punishment upon yourself."

Her breaths were coming in fast little pants. A knot stuck in her throat as she fought the alien sensation of the thing shifting, thickening and elongating inside her.

"You fucking—"

Kir muzzled her mouth with his hand, pressing his body close so that she couldn't move. "Relax. Allow the plug to conform."

I'll show you relax. Abby bit down hard on one of his fingers and tasted salt and blood on her tongue as he ripped his hand away.

The menacing growl that followed Kir's yip made her skin crawl. She was in trouble now. The tent blurred as he jerked her to her feet, spinning her around to face him. He drew her into his steely embrace. The shift in movement caused Abby to gasp as the butt-plug surged deeper.

Oh god. The thing in her ass was actually making her *hornier*!

Kir's eyes darkened. His grip tightened as his tone dropped dangerously low. "It ends here, Abby. From this point on you will not fight me. You will accept your punishments. You will subjugate to my authority. You will learn to live amongst my people as one of them." He paused and his voice turned deep and throaty. "You will be my packmate."

The finality in his voice pounded through Abby's head. He left no doubt that he had the power, the right to give commands, to enforce her obedience and to take her freedom.

No matter how she had come to care for this man, she was truly a prisoner, lost to her own world.

The back of her eyes stung, but damned if she was going to cry. Her ribs ached from lying across Kir's lap during the journey. Her body throbbed with unfulfilled desire. And her heart broke for what she wanted, but couldn't have — his love, given and shared on an equal basis.

Kir was everything she had dreamed of, but not here in this strange place, not like this.

Not as his possession.

He pinched her chin between his thumb and forefinger. "Do you understand me?"

Abby considered everything from shouting back at him, to hurting him as much as she could, to falling on the floor in a limp heap. Let him have his damned submissive. See how much he liked commanding a rag doll.

God, she hurt inside.

As his expression tightened, waiting for her answer, she came to a difficult decision.

One more time she'd play this game, and by God, she'd enjoy it all she could.

Before he got really angry she gave an answer in the form of a single nod.

The pressure of his fingers increased, biting into her cheeks. "Answer me aloud, Abby."

How she wanted to tear her face from his touch and turn away from his intense gaze. Instead she murmured, "Yes, M'Lord."

"Good. Now stand in the middle of the tent."

Without being asked a second time she moved to the location he indicated.

Your way. For now.

She felt totally weird walking with the plug in her ass.

From the thick, sturdy pole firmly holding up the tent ceiling dropped two chains with handcuffs connected to each end. Abby's heart slammed against her chest—whether from fear or excitement she wasn't sure. He was going to restrain her again. Before he could issue the command she slipped her hands into the iron rings. An act she knew Kir would read as her surrender.

The sound of steel striking steel sent chills racing across her skin. The cuffs were snug but not too tight.

Her gaze followed Kir as he strolled across the tent. He reached into a small bag lying on the bed made of furs. He withdrew his hand, fist closed, hiding something from her.

Once again Abby prepared herself for the unknown. She straightened the best she could, handcuffed to the ceiling of the tent the way she was. She raised her chin and took a deep cleansing breath. She didn't have to wait long. With determination in his steps, Kir came to her and dropped to his knees.

From his crouched position he stared up at her. "Spread your legs."

When she obeyed something cold and wet slipped inside her, but this time he inserted it in her slit. Immediately she felt the object attach itself to each swollen fold, and it began to spread her pussy wide.

The evening air whispered lightly over the inside walls of her core. The sensation of her ass filled to the brim and her pussy pried open left her feeling both filled and empty. The conflicting phenomenon tossed her body into chaos. She arched, pulling against her bindings. Her vaginal muscles struggled to close over something, anything. The impulse to press her thighs together was overwhelming as he held her legs apart.

"Please," Abby choked. A tear raced down her cheek, falling upon his upturned face. He blinked, his features softening. For a moment she thought he would relent.

Kir rose to his feet. Gently he touched the tear that had landed on his cheek. Instead of wiping it away, he rubbed it into his skin. Then he cupped her face with his palms and pressed his lips to hers. The kiss was tentative, growing in firmness as he outlined her lips with his tongue, then thrust within her warmth.

Desire swamped Abby as her body reacted and welcomed him. Her tongue wrapped around his, her body melting against his hard chest. Mewling sounds bubbled from her throat.

When they parted, he again drew her into his arms. "There is no dishonor in surrender, only in continuing to fight a losing battle. Let me take care of you, Abby." His warm breath teased the hair tucked behind her ear.

Damn him. He could almost make her believe she was truly willing to surrender.

She squirmed against him and her bonds. "Make these things stop."

He pulled away, holding her at arms' length. Laughter flickered in the depths of his blue eyes. The beginning of a smile teased the corner of his lips.

Double-damn the man.

"If it's the last thing I do, I'll prove that I won't stop fighting you." The words shot out of her mouth before she had a chance to stop them. "And that includes not letting you get to me."

"As you wish." His gaze burned into her. When he released his breath, his shoulders trembled. Was it from fury or excitement? "Once again, remember you are not to come without my permission. Should you do so, your punishment will be beyond what you can imagine."

His words were like a velvet whip striking her with doubt. She flinched but that didn't change her resolve.

"Then begin," she taunted, all the while praying for the mettle to conquer this man at least in this small way.

Her jaws clenched tight as he began to palm her breasts. His gaze locked in a silent battle with hers. Without breaking eye contact he bent and took a nipple into the warmth of his mouth. He then pulled away and blew his breath upon her wet bud. The dark ring of her areola swelled.

His heated stare, combined with the moving plug in her ass and the thing widening her pussy lips, was almost too much. Abby sucked in a ragged breath and broke the connection as her gaze darted away. She wet her lips and couldn't resist looking down at him. His eyes were fixed on her breast as he played leisurely, rubbing the pad of his finger across the raised skin as if amazed.

His tongue was moist as he lapped at her other nipple. "Mmmm... You taste wonderful. I cannot wait until you are heavy with my pups. Your ivory breasts swollen with life's nectar."

Goose bumps raced across her skin. "You promised. I- I'm not pregnant, am I?"

"Not until we are bonded in ceremony." Heavy aroused eyes met hers. "Will you allow me to taste the cream of your body?"

Her breath left her lungs in a single gush of air.

Fuck. Fuck. Fuck. This man was pushing her to the brink. Again. In a desperate act to keep from allowing him to arouse her, she sucked in the inside of her cheek and bit down hard. Pain exploded. The coppery taste of blood was strangely sweet on her tongue.

When he nibbled the tip of her nipple, her mind burst into song.

My eyes have seen the glory of the coming of the Lord. The unexpected words came loud and clear in her head—anything to curtail the heat that twisted in her belly. Like a back-draft, the fire inside her silently waited for a rush of oxygen to ignite it, to spread it out of control.

Hmm, hmm, hmm, she hummed. Damn what were the next words to the song? *He is… He is… He is. Oh shit, He is—what?* But before she could fill in the blank the man thrust his tongue in and out of her bellybutton.

Her fingers splayed wide then folded around the chains, her knuckles paling as her body jerked and went on her tiptoes.

Fight it—fight it—fight it, her mind screamed.

As if he knew the battle she waged within, he stilled his torturous tongue, granting her leniency when he rubbed his face softly against her abdomen. Prickly stubble scratched her skin. His inhale was audible as he breathed in her scent.

God, how she wanted to run her fingers through his hair, smooth her hands over the muscles of his chest. And his cock? *Well, let's not even go there.*

"Women are a gift." His calloused fingertips drew little circles upon her stomach, his gentle touch pleasing and oh-so sensuous. "And you hold the gift of life within you."

Shit. No more talk about babies. Truth was, Abby yearned for a family, craved to hold a baby to her breast, to have a man to love. She gazed down upon him. She wanted Kir. Contentment chased away the creases that only moments ago had marred his handsome features.

He offered her everything but freedom and choice. How could this man be so stern one minute and then so tender, so loving the next?

Abby's feet shuffled nervously, pulling her body away and breaking his touch in mid-stroke.

Again their gazes locked.

"You are so beautiful." His hands skimmed beneath the swollen globes of her breasts, smoothed over her stomach, dipped along the curve of her waist, before resting on her hips.

He smiled. "Your woman's core tastes of honey, of energy, of life."

Here we go again with life. Abby rolled her eyes heavenward, resisting the urge to scream.

"Shall I taste you?"

No, no, no. She would never live through that sinful torture.

Kir's head bobbed between her legs, his golden mane wild and beautiful. His breath warmed her parted folds, tickled her center and teased her with what was to come.

When finally his tongue circled her clit Abby thought she would die a million deaths. His lips closed upon the swollen bud, sucking, pulling her deeper within his hot cave. His strokes were slow, as if he savored her essence and reveled in her taste.

Abby's eyes closed. Not by choice, but by sensations. She fought the rising climax by breathing deeply, then releasing it on the count of four. Over and over she inhaled and then released it slowly. Amazingly, her orgasm was held at bay, allowing her to ride the crest, like a surfer on the swell of a breaker. She perched on the edge of madness, wanting to remain in this realm of bliss, wanting to feel the rush of sensations burning through her body.

And then nothing. Kir's touch vanished, leaving her slit throbbing, her body incomplete.

Slowly Abby opened her eyes. What reflected back was pride. It glowed upon Kir's face.

Without him saying a word Abby knew she had pleased him. And it thrilled her beyond words. She had never wanted to please a man, especially this one—until now. The gleam in his eyes was well worth her body's hunger.

"I need to fuck you," his throaty voice trembled, "now." With haste he released the object from her pussy, then with a wave of his hand the butt-plug shrank and dislodged, falling to the floor.

Kir moved behind her and she heard the click of the handcuffs, felt the iron fall away from her wrists, and then his warmth vanished from her backside. When she turned, Abby saw Kir lounging on the bed of furs, naked, his back supported by a stack of fluffy pillows. His erection surged from between his thighs, velvet-covered steel. One knee was bent, his arm resting upon it.

Abby's pulse raced with the need to feel him thrust deep within her. She didn't move. She couldn't. Her knees had turned into a mass of nothingness.

"Come to me, Abby." The sensuality of his voice, the hunger in his eyes was magnetic, giving her strength, drawing her closer and closer until she slid beside him.

"I need to feel you beneath me." He covered her with his length as he moved between her thighs. He held himself poised above her, his hands braced on either side of her. "You will not come until I give permission."

When she nodded he lowered his body until flesh was against flesh. With a single thrust he entered her.

Abby gasped. He was hard and thick and he filled her completely. A tremor shook him and she smiled, satisfied that he was affected by their joining. When he started to move in a slow, steady rhythm that threatened to break her, Abby began her new breathing technique. Small fractures of lightning stung through her core, but she held sure, surprising herself by wanting to please Kir, wanting to enhance the inevitable.

Kir thrust faster, harder. The sound of skin slapping skin, the smell of their essences mingling, became almost overwhelming. Abby prayed she could hold out.

Just as she felt the threads of control fray, Kir shouted, "Now, Abby, come for me. *Now.*"

Electricity exploded throughout her mind, her body. White-hot rays sizzled, stinging each nerve-ending, sending spasms scattering throughout her. A deep guttural moan was all the sound she could make. For a moment she couldn't breathe, trapped in the midst of release.

"Open your mouth." Abby didn't think, only obeyed. When she did, Kir slipped something upon her tongue. Immediately it began to melt and her orgasm began anew.

The taste was heavenly, like the smoothest, most exquisite chocolate, as her body was swamped with waves of deep, soul-wrenching sensations.

Arms locked around Kir, she trembled when his muscles bunched and he threw back his head and howled. The sound was beautiful as it was joined by others from somewhere close. The howls of wolves and the roar of tigers.

Sated, Kir moved from atop Abby, pulling her into his arms. The light in the tent flickered and he smiled.

"What?" Abby looked into his eyes.

His mischievous grin made him look younger, a boyish expression that drew her closer into his embrace. "See our shadows enlarged against the walls of the tent?"

Abby nodded.

"Our comrades have seen the silhouettes of all that has occurred within this tent. Their joined voices were approval of my choice of packmate."

A flush of heat erupted across Abby's cheeks as she remembered the camping trips she had been on in the past, and how shadows could be seen within a lighted tent. The canvas must have hidden nothing from onlookers—or voyeurs in this case. Abby didn't know if it angered or excited her to know that the entire scouting party had watched them fucking.

"Should we respond by indulging ourselves once more?" he asked, already pulling her atop him.

Abby didn't stop him. Instead she went willingly and was surprised when he maneuvered her so that her slit faced him and they were in a sixty-nine position.

"I want to see how much you enjoy taking me into your mouth while I take you in mine." His hands smoothed up the inside of her thighs, spreading her wider.

Abby's nervously glanced toward her shadow reflecting off the canvas. She watched the dark shape of Kir's hands stroking her legs. Then she looked down at the evidence of his arousal and licked her lips.

When her fingers closed around his shaft, he sucked in a throaty breath. "Yes," he whispered. "Spread your thighs wider and arch your back." She moved in position. "So beautiful. So wet. I want to drive you to climax again until you scream. Drop your chest so that I can feel your nipples scrape my belly as you take me into your mouth."

The position spread her wide for Kir's delight and teased her tight buds. It also made an exciting picture reflecting back to her off the walls of the tent. Abby gasped as she stole one last look before taking Kir deep into her mouth.

As she began to stroke his cock with her tongue, Kir parted her slit with his thumbs. In circular motions he worked her body back into a frenzy. Kir raised his head to taste her juices, sending tremors surging through Abby.

Oh, God. He was going to kill her again. "May I come, M'Lord?"

"Yes, my love, you have earned your pleasure." He sucked her clit into his mouth, his tongue flicking against the sensitive bud.

Abby screamed. Wave after wave of vibrations filtered through her body as Kir drank from her. When the sensations became too much she tried to pull away.

"No more, I can't take any more." She squirmed, hoping that he would cease while praying he never would.

With a low growl he turned her and crawled beside her, gently pressing his length against hers. He snuggled next to her as if he couldn't get close enough. They were skin to skin, and still Abby got the feeling it wasn't enough, even for him. When he threw a leg over her thighs, pinning her, he finally settled down. Within moments she heard his breathing deepen, felt his body relax.

"Never leave me, Abby. Promise you will never leave me." The words were almost inaudible as he sank deeper into slumber.

One tear fell, then another and another until a stream ran down her cheeks.

She didn't answer him.

Thank God he didn't notice.

After all he had said tonight, after all she had realized, she had no choice but to leave.

She'd gone and lost her heart to this man, but she'd be damned if she was going to lose her freedom too.

Chapter Sixteen

🔊

Air crackled with Balin's anger. The wolf had fucked the woman all night long and the sorcerer could do nothing but watch from his crystal ball. Fury laced his veins with red-hot fire as her image cried for the wolf.

The woman was weak.

Weak as all humans.

The thought brought his fiery gaze from the crystal toward the naked man chained to the stone wall. He hung limp, a rag doll, torn and bruised.

This man had called himself John Steele, once husband of the now Queen of Clubs. He had offered his services in bringing the King of Clubs to his knees as long as his prize was Awai. The man had shimmered with hatred for the bitch. A hatred Balin knew all too well.

But Steele was human, a lesser being. Balin's long fingers curled into fists. To accept his assistance would be admitting weakness in his own power. He could not allow his people to question him.

Balin gave a slow and satisfied smile. He had used his mind-control to destroy the *bakirs* locked in Lord Kir's dungeons. Using Abby's mind, he was able to get close enough, and it had taken only a single push at a werewolf guard's thoughts to make him unlock one of the *bakir's* chains. Then as the mesmerized wolf stumbled up the stairs, back to his post, Balin released the madness of the *bakir* among his comrades and they had ripped one another apart.

The blood lust that reigned in the cells had turned Balin's attention toward Steele.

Balin made his way to Steele. Balin's blood-stained white robe swirled around his ankles with each step before he stopped in front of Steele. With one finger beneath the man's chin he raised his head. His eyes were swollen shut and dried blood made a path from his mouth to his throat.

Balin's finger dropped from beneath Steele's chin and the man's head bobbed against his chest.

For a while the human had been great entertainment. Balin had bound Steele's cock and balls with a coarse twine, then whipped him repeatedly. The infidel had screamed like a banshee. Yet the ultimate enjoyment was when Balin removed the man's chains and dropped him to his hands and knees. The sorcerer had driven his own cock into the man's tight anus, pounding into Steele until Balin found his own release. The man had obviously been fucked in the ass before and the sorcerer wondered if the human had found pleasure at the invasion. At one point it had occurred to Balin that the man seemed to enjoy his torture to some degree.

Balin turned from the man in disgust. This human was only a shell. Not worthy of his further attention. When Steele woke from his unconsciousness he would be fed to Balin's *bakirs*.

The crystal ball blazed a fluorescent blue, drawing Balin's attention back to it.

It was time.

The quartz perched on a large granite desk before a set of mammoth windows that looked out upon Balin's realm. But his attention was only for the crystal as a scene unfolded before him. Abby cuddled within Lord Kir's arms, a soft smile of pleasure on her beautiful features.

In a heated fury Balin swiped his hand across the tabletop, barely missing the seeing stone. He sent everything else flying into the air. A glass shattered against the wall, paper scattered about, and the wine decanter crashed to the floor. It spilled rich, red wine like blood pouring onto the flagstones.

He trembled and attempted to rein in his control. He needed something to relax him, someone to ease his suffering.

"Azu!"

A small petite blonde rushed into the room. In her haste she fell when coming in contact with the spilled wine and slid across the room, stopping at Balin's feet. When she made to rise, he grasped her shoulder and shoved her back against the floor.

He grabbed a handful of her hair, which was something the woman enjoyed. He jerked her so that she was on her haunches. "There is no need for you to stand. Your task is better done on your knees." He forced her face down on his bulging groin. "Suck my cock, wench, and be quick at it."

When she parted his robe and took him into her mouth he released a heavy breath. With a thrust of his hips he drove his penis down her throat and smiled as her eyes began to water. The little gurgling sounds she made as she choked pleased him. Yet he knew she felt pleasure too. The wench enjoyed being used in whatever fashion he chose.

Immediately he felt more in control, more himself. While the wench gave him pleasure he ran his hand over the cool crystal.

"Wake, my pretty, it is time."

The woman within the glass whimpered. Abby twisted as if his call was more a nightmare than the escape it was meant to be. Or what he had given her to believe.

"Wake, my pretty," he repeated as he felt his climax building. His hand wound in the blonde's hair, jerking her face back so that their gazes met. "Faster, bitch, I don't have time to tarry." He twisted his hand, tightening his hold.

With that the woman forced his large cock down her throat. She gagged, the muscles in her neck squeezing him, closing around him until his seed released in a fiery discharge. It was in those moments that he felt a bit of his control shattering with each wave of his orgasm.

No. He never lost control. Teeth clenched tight, Balin hissed as he pulled from the woman's mouth.

"Get out of here," he growled as he cupped himself. She didn't even try to rise, but crawled from the room, her gaze darting to the man hanging from the wall. Gently, Balin's hand slid from the base to the tip of his erection. That had been good. Very good. With a sigh of satisfaction he let his robe fall back over his now-flaccid cock.

It was time.

All it took was a simple mental command and a team of his black-robed *bakirs* were saddling their beasts. They would snatch Abby once he had her far enough from the encampment.

When he again gazed into the crystal, Abby was in a sitting position. The sappy look on her face as she stared down at Lord Kir was enough to make Balin growl. The bitch had no taste.

Still he lowered his mental voice. *Ah, you are awake,* he said to her in mind-thought.

"Balin," she murmured gazing about the tent.

Hush, my pretty, you mustn't wake the beast. It is time. The scouting party sleeps and I am near.

"But—"

He broke her train of thought by interjecting a picture of her farm, a scene he had taken from her memories. She gasped as her stupid dog, then a puppy, poked its head from the basket her Uncle Henry carried. When Abby began to sob the scene vanished. The last thing he needed was her to rouse the werewolf beside her.

It is time to go, Abby. Are you ready? When she hesitated he added, *Your aunt awaits you. Did you know she is not well? No, you would not, being held prisoner against your will. I believe she has a weak heart. Time is of the essence.*

Abby's palm covered her mouth as she muffled her cry. Carefully she slipped from Kir's embrace. She stopped once to touch the wolf's mane with such gentleness that Balin released a growl. Her head snapped up and a wisp of fear widened her eyes as she hurried to her feet.

The sound was only one of the wolves dreaming. Now come to me.

On feather-light feet she moved across the tent, silently raised the flap and stepped into the night.

The chill beaded her nipples and Balin stifled another growl. He would pierce those nipples and hang his badge of ownership from each one. Lord Kir would be there to watch while he fucked the woman. He could picture the rage on Kir's face as he struggled against his bonds, even as Balin's cock drove further into Abby's core.

Just the thought made his member lengthen, harden. Balin gave a wicked smile. After killing Kir, the sorcerer might even take the wolf's dick as a trophy to hang from his mantle.

O stirred as Abby walked past him. Balin frowned.

Leave the dog. He will only hinder your escape, he ordered Abby.

"I can't." Her voice was tight with emotion.

You must for your aunt's sake. He knew he'd said the right thing as she began to move through the camp.

Damn. The woman had shit for brains. She was headed the wrong direction.

Turn around, my pretty. You must hurry toward the cluster of trees to your left. Balin shot an image of himself dressed in leather pants, his dark hair flowing upon the breeze, his hand outstretched. *Come to me. Let me lead you home.*

Abby moved past all the sleeping tigers and wolves. He saw her hesitate as a guard sniffed the air. *He is immune to your scent. Plus you carry the scent of his master.* The fact made a nerve tick in Balin's neck. *He will not interfere. Just be cautious.*

Of course no one would notice Abby leaving, but he needn't tell her that little fact. Balin had encompassed her in a mental bubble of protection that shrouded her scent and her body. Even her footsteps would be masked.

At least the bitch could follow orders. She moved carefully, darting behind a bush and avoiding the guard's sight.

The night was clear and a bright moon seeped through the forest canopy to guide the woman. Once she stumbled and fell, but she picked herself up without a sound and continued. It was curious how this woman still had feelings for an aunt who obviously had treated Abby poorly. Foolish.

At the same time Abby made her way toward his trap he sensed his *bakirs* closing in on her. Not much longer and she would be his. And she would be the ruin of Kir.

Then all hell broke loose.

A single wolf's cry rent the air.

Abby came to a dead halt. She whipped around. She took one step, grasping the area above her left breast, almost as if the cry pierced her heart.

The leader of that damnable pack was awake.

Without delay Balin sent another imagine of Abby's aunt.

Run, my pretty. The wolves are after you! Flee toward the ocean of red.

Chapter Seventeen

ജ

Kir's cry had been filled with pain. Abby sensed no anger, but a deep, hollow emptiness. For a moment she had thought to return. But when the image of Aunt Maye flashed in her mind she turned the other direction. Her aunt was sick, maybe dying, and the old woman was alone. The thought made Abby take one step, then another, until she hit a run.

The moment she left the treeline she saw the ocean of red. A field of poppies so tall they nearly reached her shoulders. Balin's voice drew her to the blooms like a magnet. The closer she got to the flowers the stronger their sweet scent grew. The smell was overpowering. She staggered as she entered the field of flowers.

Again she heard Kir call to her. She didn't need to speak wolf to know he was calling her home.

Home. The thought was eerie and comforting at the same time. Could she make a home with Kir here in this strange land?

No. She needed to get back to Aunt Maye, needed to make sure her aunt was all right. She stumbled forward, going deeper and deeper into the tall poppies.

In Abby's mind's eye Balin raised his arms to the sky. He was beautiful against the dark of night.

I call upon the winds from the north to blow cold and hard.

Immediately gusts of air whirled the soft petals of the flowers, picking up their seeds, spreading their scent of poppies over the land. The currents like sharp needles pelting Abby back, literally pushing her. She tried to stop, thought of asking Kir to send her back to Kansas on a promise she would return, but the winds fought her — drove her forward.

Abby blinked hard, her eyes blurring, burning. The scent of poppies was overpowering and forced air from her lungs in a rush. She tried to hold her breath but failed. With every breath she sucked pollen into her lungs. In slow motion, her knees hit the ground. Small black seeds burst from the center of the poppies as she fell upon them. Her body went limp. She twisted and managed to fall on her back, crushing stems and flowers beneath her.

What was happening? She attempted to raise her arm, but it remained motionless at her side. Horrified, she lay paralyzed as dead and dying leaves rose into the air. They twirled in a tornado that skimmed the tips of the flowers before dropping petals and leaves upon her one at a time. One, then two, then dozens, followed by hundreds.

Her mind screamed in fear. She was being buried alive.

She tried to open her mouth, tried cry out to Kir, but nothing happened. Leaves and petals began to cover her face. She was helpless to brush them aside. And she knew there was no way Kir would find her before she suffocated.

Evil laughter stabbed her cocoon. *Sleep*, Balin said, and his tone was filled with menace she'd never heard in his voice before. *Sleep and when you wake I will have a surprise for you.*

Abby struggled to maintain consciousness. But she had no choice except to obey as she drifted into darkness.

Chapter Eighteen

🕉

The pain in Kir's chest knifed so deeply he was nearly immobilized by it. He knew she was gone—and not just gone. Kir knew Abby had left him.

But why? Why the very night she had at last given herself to him? She had trusted him with her pleasure, wanted him, seemed to love him—and she stole away without so much as a proper farewell.

Why?

Because she knew I would never let her go. She knew I would have forced her to stay. Gods, what kind of man am I that I would have to force my true packmate to remain with me against her will?

"I gave her more than I've given any woman," he argued aloud, trying to battle the pain. "I gave her everything."

Everything but what she wanted, he answered himself...in a voice that sounded remarkably like that of one of the Tarok Queens. In fact, the exact words of Alexi, Queen of Spades, rang through his mind.

She may not ever submit the way you want her to. It isn't natural for her.

Abby enjoyed submission, she craved it, loved it, even—but in her heart, she could not submit in all aspects of her life. It wasn't natural for her, it wasn't what she wanted.

He, Kir, was not what she wanted—not if his love came at the price of her freedom. Her independence meant that much to her.

Images of Alexi and Mikaela played in his mind. Yes. Those women were much the same.

He had been so certain of himself, so against the compromises King Darronn of Spades had been willing to make to win his mate.

Why did those concessions seem so insignificant now?

"Damn me." His unwillingness to be flexible, his attempt to trap Abby's spirit within his control, had driven her away from him. "Damn everything!"

He could not let her go.

He wouldn't.

Not without telling her of his love. Not without speaking his regrets and giving her the choice to stay with him and promising her that she would always have her freedom. He would not force her to submit to him unless she wished to. It would always be her choice. It should have been from the start.

Even greater pain laced Kir's heart as he howled again. He shifted from man to wolf until he was on all fours and golden fur covered his body. As he transformed, every wolf, every weretiger and even the werefin answered his call. Their responses told him they would help him find Abby and bring her safely back to him.

Kir rushed out of his tent, barking orders to his captains. He commanded most to stay. They needed to guard the camp and protect the other women. It would not do to allow Balin or Steele this opportunity to catch them unaware. The headstrong Alexi tried to join in on the search but was convinced by her mate to stay and help guard her pregnant aunt Awai.

Members of the search team caught Abby's scent in the encampment, but it went no further than the few paces she had made last night.

How could that be?

"It is as if she has vanished completely," Prince Eral muttered in his man form from his mount. He was riding bareback on one of the *jul.* As a werefin, Eral was most comfortable in the water, but his senses remained sharp, even on land. From his shoulder hung his crossbow and a quiver of arrows.

No tree holds her scent, King Darronn said in mind-speak and he gave a low growl. *I do not believe she escaped that way.*

Then how? Kir responded, his heart pounding so hard that his chest ached even more. His keen eyes searched the ground for signs of Abby. A footprint. A broken twig. Anything that would lead them to her.

Fan out, Kir ordered his men as well as the prince and the kings. *We must find her.*

Before Balin does.

The moment the thought entered Kir's mind, blood throbbed in his head and sudden fear rushed to his heart.

Make haste! he commanded.

Kir loped forward along the forest path, trying to catch Abby's scent. He had never felt so helpless. His senses were blinded to her. He tried to block out the sound of squirrels chittering in the trees, the calls of night birds, the dash of rabbits through the bushes. Tried to ignore the scents of the other were-beings, the rich smell of the earth, the odor of pine and *ch'tok* trees. Tried to concentrate only on some sign of Abby.

Everything seemed to be at work against him, as if angered at how he had treated the woman he loved.

He heard a sharp bark and glanced over his shoulder to see O bounding after him. He sensed the animal's concern for his mistress and his single-mindedness in finding her. The same single-mindedness that Kir had in retrieving his woman.

Kir picked up his speed, darting along the path toward the treeline. Beyond the trees was a grassy meadow that stretched for acres. He sniffed the air and caught an unfamiliar scent—a scent that did not belong in his realm. A smell that sent chills throughout his furred body.

When he burst out of the wood he saw them. He came up short while O continued on, charging past him.

Red flowers—poppies—that seemed to go on forever. They glistened under the moonlight like a sea of blood. Where could the blooms have come from?

A cold fist gripped his heart.

Balin.

Kir howled to his comrades, calling them to him even as he loped toward the flowers, following O. The sickly-sweet odor of the poppies was nearly overpowering, wiping out his ability to scent anything but the red blooms.

Before he entered the flowers, on the dark horizon beneath the moon's glow, he saw and heard them. Dark-cloaked figures riding hideous beasts that snarled as they galloped into the poppies from the opposite side.

Bakirs.

Kir howled again, alerting his people to the danger and the presence of the sorcerer's minions. Calling to the rest of the hunting party to hurry to him.

Kir's gaze riveted on a break in the sea of flowers, as if someone had made a weak trail through the red blooms. It had to have been Abby—and Balin must have sent the *bakirs* to capture her.

But how could the sorcerer know of Abby? Why would she go to Balin?

The answer came to him even as he darted into poppies. *He must have used some kind of mind control.*

Again he cursed his own asinine rigidity. He'd wounded her with his pride. He'd broken her heart and left her vulnerable.

O and Kir both growled as they plowed down the flowers. The Irish wolfhound stumbled, shook his head, then continued. Kir felt the power of the poppies attempting to capture his senses. His mind felt muddled as pollen dashed into his eyes and across his muzzle. O stumbled again and slowed, moving in a strange motion, as if he could barely lift his legs.

Kir charged past the dog, refusing to let the dark magic of the blooms overcome him. His own legs felt weak. His vision blurred and he could barely see where the blooms were trampled ahead. The poppies were over his head and he couldn't see the *bakirs*, but he knew they were coming. Sensed them. Heard the pounding of the beasts' hooves. Felt the *bakirs'* mental ambush.

Like a trail of sunshine lighting the darkness, through the thick smell of the poppies Kir caught Abby's sweet scent of woman. In the next moment he nearly stumbled over her body. She was buried beneath leaves and petals. Without pause he shifted into a man, his body elongating, his forepaws becoming hands that quickly shoved the debris from her face.

An anguished cry tore from his lips as he saw how deathly white she was beneath the bright moonlight. "Abby!" he shouted as he brushed away the last of the petals. "Wake, my love."

She didn't move. Her chest didn't even rise with the barest of breaths.

Kir was hardly conscious himself. He struggled to maintain control over his limbs as he lowered his mouth to Abby's. He cupped the back of her head. Pressed his lips to hers. Blew air into her lungs. When she didn't respond, he did it again. Then twice more.

Abby choked. Coughed up a few poppy petals. Sucked in a deep breath and her lashes fluttered. Relief flooded Kir that she was alive, yet at the same time terror rose that they might be captured by the *bakirs* and taken to Balin. Not terror for himself, but fear for Abby. Gods, how he could not bear to have anything happen to his woman, his love.

He felt a thud at his feet and his blurry gaze saw that O had collapsed at his mistress's side.

Kir's vision swam. His arms and legs became lead. His body slumped next to Abby, and he fell into a deep and mindless sleep.

Chapter Nineteen

🔖

Using his crystal globe, Balin gave a triumphant smile as he watched Kir's fall. The sorcerer's *bakirs* were almost to the bastard and his bitch. Due to Balin's mental powers, the *bakirs* were insensitive to the magic of the blooms and would be able to retrieve the werewolf and the woman with no trouble. The beasts they rode would be used to carry the bodies of Kir and Abby back to Malachad.

Balin even sent a mind-command for the *bakirs* to take the dog as well. From what he had learned of Abby, she would be split in two—given the choice of her love for her pet and her love for the wolf—when he made her choose which of them would die first. Werewolf or dog.

The sorcerer's grin turned into a glare at the thought of the woman actually loving the wolf. The fucking werewolf who had helped the Tarok kings free Mikaela, the sorcerer's former bitch of a queen. Balin clenched his fists so tightly that his nails dug into the flesh of his palms and blood seeped past his fingernails and splattered onto his white robe. The coppery scent of his own life's fluid only made him hungrier for Kir's and Abby's, for the revenge he would have when they were brought to him.

Mikaela had been Balin's most powerful ally. She would have destroyed the Tarok brothers, leaving Balin to pillage their kingdoms and gain the power he hungered to possess. But all had been ruined by the kings, their new queens and Kir. Mikaela had slipped from Balin's mental grasp. The traitorous bitch had aligned herself once more with her brothers. He trembled, refusing to admit he felt anything but hatred for the woman.

Lord Kir had been among those who helped to free her.

And he would be one of the first to die.

Balin took a deep breath and watched with satisfaction as his *bakirs* neared the inert forms of Kir and Abby.

Something shimmered through the night, like a horizontal bolt of lightning. It flew so quickly that Balin barely saw it before the deadly arrow struck one of the *bakirs*.

"No!" Balin shouted even as he saw the *bakir* fly to the ground, heard the *bakir's* mental scream, felt the last throb of his dying heart.

Another arrow and another sliced through the night, driving into the hearts of the beasts and the *bakirs* upon their backs. Balin was helpless to stop the barrage of arrows as each of his *bakirs* fell into the sea of poppies. Finally only one *bakir* remained upon his beast and they were mere feet from Kir and Abby.

Trample them! Balin mind-shouted. If he could not retrieve his prizes he would at least see them murdered. *Kill them!*

But just as the beast's hooves neared Lord Kir's head, another arrow zinged through the air and lodged in the beast's heart. It reared up with one final scream, at the same time another arrow pierced the last *bakir* between the eyes.

Both beast and *bakir* tumbled to the ground, skidding within inches of the wolf and the woman.

With a roar of fury, Balin snatched a dagger from where it lay upon the table, intent on piercing Steele's heart with it—but to his unbelieving eyes the man was gone. The chains hung limply from the walls.

How could that be?

Another scream of fury and the sorcerer flung the dagger with all his might through the open doorway, not caring where it landed.

A scream and then a soft thud.

Azu slid from the darkness into the moonlight slanting through the tall windows of the tower. Blood formed a shimmering black pool as it poured from her body where the dagger had driven into her chest.

Rage flooded Balin in a rush so powerful the tower windows exploded. Glass rained down, inside and out of the tower.

Now his favorite plaything was dead, he had lost many of his *bakir*, Kir and the woman, and even Steele had escaped.

His gaze riveted back on the crystal ball to see who had ruined all for him this night.

Prince Eral, the werefin, sat astride the back of a *jul*. He held a crossbow as his beast advanced through the blooms, obviously prepared to strike down any *bakir* that might still live.

Balin ground his teeth.

Of course. The werefin was of the sea, utterly unaffected by the poppies, by any magic of plants grown on dry land.

The flames of Balin's rage and hatred nearly consumed him.

Another arrogant bastard. Another target.

Blood dripped and flowed around the King of Malachad. He had one clear thought, and only one.

Prince Eral would pay.

Chapter Twenty

ॐ

It had been three days and Kir had not left Abby's side, yet still she remained unconscious. Once Prince Eral and the other werefins had retrieved Abby, O and Kir from the poisonous poppies, they had made haste back to Emerald City and to the healer Linara. All of them had been taken to the healing waters at once, and the toxic pollens had been cleansed.

O had woken just hours later and had stayed at Abby's side until Kir woke the following day. Kir had demanded to see Abby at once. She had been brought to him and settled beside him in his bed where she remained until this very moment. O had insisted on taking up vigil beside the bed, only leaving to eat and to relieve himself when Linara dragged the dog from the room.

And still Abby slept.

Her auburn hair lay in wild waves around her beautiful fae features.

Linara believed Abby would wake soon, that her body simply needed to recover from the trauma of the experience. Yet Kir couldn't help but fear for his kitten. He wanted her back, claws and all. He would do anything she wanted, anything at all, so long as she came back to him.

He raked his fingers through his hair and paced the large bedchamber, his feet sinking into the wall-to-wall white carpet. Abby lay upon his bed within the enormous hulled-out boulder that was filled with pillows, blankets and downy-soft furs. Her sweet scent of woman and the healing oils that had been applied to her skin mingled with the fresh clean smell of the chamber.

Prince Eral had more than fulfilled his oath to Kir and would soon return to Atlantis. Kir had long ago insisted the man owed him no obligation, but the pride of the werefin people was great. Eral had refused to leave Kir's service until the debt was repaid.

Eral had saved Kir and Abby, not to mention Abby's beloved pet, O. It was Kir's turn to owe a great debt to the prince.

The ever-present rush of the natural shower behind the emerald wall matched the rush in Kir's blood when he saw Abby move and heard her soft moan. He hurried to her side, knelt next to the bed and took one of her hands in his.

"Are you all right, my love?" Kir pleaded as he brought her hand to his mouth and kissed her knuckles.

Abby's eyelashes fluttered. Eyes still closed, she pressed the palm of her free hand to her forehead. "Damn that must have been one hell of a party," she muttered. "A hunky werewolf? I'm never drinking tequila again."

Kir smiled and lowered his face to brush his lips against Abby's. "This is no dream, love. You are where you belong. At my side."

Her eyelids flew open and Kir rose so that he was no longer leaning over her. She quickly pushed herself to a sitting position. For one moment she looked pale and held her head in her hands.

"Are you all right, kitten?" Fear raised the hair at Kir's nape. "I will get the healer at once."

"No." She reached out and grabbed his hand before he could move away. "I-I'm fine. I've just got a friggin' headache." She took a deep breath and he could see color return to her face as her cinnamon eyes met his. "Don't leave me, okay?"

Kir couldn't help a smile. "I will never leave you, my love."

Abby's grip on his hand tightened and her eyes widened. "What did you say?"

He reached up with his free hand and brushed a heavy fall of her auburn hair away from her face. He couldn't help but lean forward and press his lips to the faerie kisses on her nose.

When he leaned back she was still staring at him with wide eyes. "What's going on here?"

"I love you, Abby of Kanzaz." The word was still strange on his tongue as he caught her chin in his hand. "I ask you to be my packmate, freely, by your own choice—and your own rules. I want you to be with me always as my equal."

Chapter Twenty-One

සා

Abby couldn't breathe. She couldn't think. Had Kir declared his love? Had he asked, not demanded, her to stay? And not as a lesser partner, but an equal?

Before she could speak, there was a light tap on the door. Both Kir and Abby looked toward it and then at each other. Anxiety flickered in the depths of his eyes. Clearly neither wanted to be disturbed at this precious moment.

Then the tap turned into a pound and the door burst open. Alexi entered, her auburn hair flowing around her face. She was dressed again in a sexy leather halter and pants that showed off every curve.

Kir's hand slipped from Abby's face. Annoyance plastered his features. Abby drew the linens up and over her lap to cover her breasts. Kir didn't bother to cover himself.

Alexi glanced back at her aunt Awai who followed. "Abby's awake. I knew she would be."

With ease Awai sat on the corner of the bed, on the other side of Kir, her full breasts brimming from the loose white robe she wore. With a smile she clasped her hands around one of Abby's. "Thank God you're okay."

Just then the Kings of Spades and Clubs entered the room, dwarfing the space with their mere presence. Heavy footsteps echoed their anger as each moved next to their mates.

With a deep bow, Ty began to apologize, "Pardon our intrusion, Lord Kir." The man pinned his wife with a heated glare. "Apparently our women do not care what punishment will be inflicted, since they did not heed our warning to leave you alone."

Awai frowned and attempted to move away from her husband's hand as it rested firmly on her shoulder.

Alexi's stance grew rigid. She nudged her chin higher, cocked a brow and shot her husband a silent dare.

Shaking his head, Darronn rolled his eyes. Then he drew a reluctant Alexi into his arms. It took only a moment for the woman to soften into the man's embrace.

"I should spank you until you cannot sit for a week," the King of Spades muttered close to Alexi's ear.

"Promise?" she teased, but yelped when the man's hand landed on her leather-clad ass.

Yeah, from the besotted expressions on both the imposing kings' faces, their women were more likely to be loved and cherished to death, instead of punished for disobedience.

Abby turned and saw the same tender emotion in Kir's eyes as he gazed upon her. He loved her. He truly, truly loved her.

From the hallway a woman squealed. A bark and a growl of warning followed. Chaos reigned as O burst through the open door. Linara, breathing heavily, was hot on his heels. Before she could grab the leash trailing behind O, the huge Irish wolfhound lunged, soaring through the air and practically landing on top of Abby.

Damn that animal. Still Abby couldn't help the laughter bubbling from her throat. She had never been so happy to see the troublesome dog. As she petted his back, he licked her face then settled down, laying his head on her sheet-covered lap.

The rise and fall of the healer's large, naked chest caught the eyes of every man in the room. In unconscious unison,

Abby, Alexi and Awai swung out, striking each of their men on the shoulders with an open palm. And, as if choreographed, each man yipped, "Oww!"

The innocent expression on Kir's face warmed Abby. He truly wasn't interested in Linara. He wanted *her*, Dorothy Abigail Osborne of Kansas.

Linara's heavy lashes drifted down, hiding her reaction to the men's stares. But the beginnings of a grin gave her away. "I am sorry, M'Lord." Her chest rose and fell rapidly. Perhaps a little too fast. "The dog seemed to know his mistress had regained consciousness. He would not be restrained." Then she smiled, bowing her head. "M'lady, I trust you are feeling better."

"Much better. Thank you."

"What do you wish for me to do with that animal?" Linara's frustration was directed toward O with a frown.

Darronn said, "Perhaps we should take our leave."

"But we haven't spoken with Abby," insisted Alexi.

"Later." Darronn grasped his woman by the arm.

"But—"

"Later," he growled. Alexi gave a huff but turned and made for the door. The King and Queen of Clubs followed.

Linara grabbed O's leash and gave a pull that nearly jerked her off her feet as O braced himself on the bed. It took Linara and Kir both to get the dog to the floor. Once they did, he planted his ass on the ground. With a grunt of determination Linara scooted and dragged the dog out the door, closing it softly behind them, but not before Abby heard her murmur, "Damn dog."

With that, the room emptied, leaving Abby and Kir alone. There was an awkward silence, a moment of unease that lingered. Abby couldn't help but gather the covers tighter around her, a frivolous attempt to feel a sense of security.

Kir stopped her hand with his. "Please do not hide your body from my eyes. I gain great pleasure in looking at you." The boyish smile she had only seen once before warmed her. She let the linen slide away, baring her naked breasts to his lustful eyes.

As if he couldn't resist, he reached out, palming her full ivory globes. His touch was tender, almost cherishing.

"Kitten," he paused, "I asked you to be my mate. To live with me for eternity and share my life."

Abby knew he could feel her heart thudding against her chest, beneath his hand. The moment of reprieve was over. He expected an answer.

Her body screamed, *yes*. Her heart and soul joined in.

But what about Aunt Maye? Her aunt needed her.

"Kir?" A wealth of uncertainty hung on every letter of his name.

He placed a single finger against her lips. "Touch," he whispered, "is said to be the food of our souls. Will you let me touch you, Abby?"

"Yes." She breathed deeply, her body already tingling with desire. If she couldn't have him for eternity, she would have him for the moment.

Strong hands softened as he cupped her hand in his. Just the warmth and presence of his skin on hers was comforting. With sweeping, gliding motions he moved from her wrist to her elbow and back again, stretching her forearm muscles, massaging her. He woke every nerve ending with his gentle ministrations. Without pausing, he repeated the sensual kneading on the inner side of her arm.

Again, he took her hand in his. From knuckles to wrist, he worked her joints. The massage was so relaxing. He studied her, clearly watching for any sign of pain. Funny, but he had no idea his touch could never hold discomfort, only the strength and love she craved. As if he felt as she did, he turned her hand and kissed the inside of her wrist. No words could describe the connection between them.

When his knuckles began to make small semicircular motions over her entire palm, she groaned aloud. She wanted to close her eyes, to wallow in the blissful sensation, but she was trapped in his intense gaze, trapped in the web he was weaving around her.

Then he sandwiched her hand between his and briskly rubbed back and forth, creating friction and a heat that burned through her body like wildfire. She wanted him now. Needed to feel him inside her, breathing life back into her starving soul.

With her free hand she reached for him, but he shook his head. His nostrils flared. His jaw clenched in determination. Clearly, he wasn't finished driving her crazy as he repeated the same massage to her other arm and hand.

When Abby was sure she couldn't take any more, he moved to her feet. Rotating his thumb joints, he applied pressure into his fingers so that one followed another in small, alternating circles over the sole of her foot. He played with her toes, slipping one into his mouth, sucking, moving his tongue around and around.

Abby hissed in a breath and arched her back. She hadn't known there were erogenous zones in the foot. The glimmer in his eyes told her he knew exactly what he was doing to her.

With slow movements, he smoothed his strong hands down her calf and foreleg. Firmly but gently, he swept over her kneecap, up the length of her leg. As he reached her upper thigh, he slid his fingers to the crease between her pussy and her thigh. His fingertips were a breath away from her moist core, while his other hand encircled her hip, massaging the soft skin before sliding down her thigh.

Abby whimpered when his other hand joined in the glide down her leg.

"Kir." His name was a plea upon her tongue. She tried to spread her legs wider, but he halted her with a firm grip.

"Shhh, I'm not finished." Had she ever noticed the sexual tension in his tone? The raw need in his deep voice? This man, who could shapeshift into a wolf—who ruled the lands as far as she could see—loved her.

He lifted her leg, bending it at the knee so that it touched her chest. The movement opened and spread her wide, and her toes curled in sheer ecstasy. The muscles in her pussy twitched. The palms of her hands curled into the linens.

Kir's gaze was riveted on her swollen folds. As he maneuvered her leg down and reached for the other one, his tongue slid across his lips, the sensual motion causing another wave of desire to dampen her thighs. He blinked hard, as if trying to break the trance as her foot touched the bedding.

When his gaze rose, their eyes met and electricity crackled between them. His breathing was labored as his palms gripped her hips and he moved her down the bed. Then he crawled to the head of the bed, crossed his legs Indian-style and placed her head into his lap so that she was staring up at the glittering emerald ceiling. She heard his tight inhale as her hair flowed across his cock, covering both it and his balls. He hardened even more, pulsing against the nape of her neck. The throaty groan that slipped from his throat made her giggle.

"Be quiet, woman." The command fell short as he leaned forward and kissed her forehead, before raising her head once more and slipping a pillow between their bodies. Then he glided both his hands behind her neck. Light fingertips smoothed the skin from her shoulders, along her neck to her hairline. At the base of her skull he applied pressure, his fingertips lifting her head slightly upward to give her neck a stretch. The restraint inside her snapped.

"Kir, I need to taste you." She felt like she was going to die if she didn't touch him. "Please."

Soft laughter met her plea. "So be it. It is your turn."

Abby didn't hesitate to roll over and climb upon her knees. She faced Kir, frowning at the pillow that hid his groin from her sight. He crossed his arms over his broad shoulders, hiking a brow as if to say, "What are you going to do now?"

Without hesitation she unveiled him, throwing the pillow across the room. It hit the wall with a soft thud before tumbling to the floor.

Her breath caught. "Kir, you're so beautiful."

His cock jerked beneath her appraisal.

He was steel draped in velvet as her index fingertip circled his crown. A drop of pre-come glistened from his slit. She dipped her head at the same time she stretched her body along the cool linen. When she swiped her tongue over the head of his cock, Kir shuddered, the tremor moving through Abby as she took him deep into her mouth.

"Wait." He uncurled his legs and spread them wide. He stuffed several pillows behind his back and reclined. "Fuck me with your mouth."

With pleasure, Abby wanted to say, but already Kir's hand was on the back of her head, driving her down. With slow, smooth strokes she moved from the base of his cock to the tip, swirling her tongue so that she captured his juices. Tilting her head, she caught Kir's darkened gaze. He smiled then lifted his hips.

"I love watching you fuck me with your mouth." His fingers tightened in her hair.

The subtle pain was a welcome sensation as Abby glided her teeth carefully over him. She scraped her fingernails from his armpits, down the side of his chest, to his thighs. Goose bumps skittered across his flesh and she smiled around his cock.

She sucked harder, increasing the rhythm, needing to feel Kir lose control. The pressure on her head, the rise of his hips told her he was close.

Kir cautiously extracted himself from between her lips. "Slow down. Not yet." His words were terse, as if he held onto sanity by a thread. "Crawl up here and place your thighs over mine."

Without hesitation Abby did as Kir requested.

Straddling him opened her wide, spreading her wet folds. His cock jerked, rubbing generously across her swollen lips. She placed her palms on his shoulders, dying for the moment he would thrust inside her.

Instead of entering her, he pulled her into his arms, drawing her against his chest. Together they held one another and breathed. For how long Abby didn't know, but when their heartbeats melted into one, she was lost in rapture, pure and raw.

The moment was so surreal her eyes dampened with moisture. "Make love to me." It was a whisper of deep desire, an ache burning in her soul.

Kir's hands smoothed over her back and rested on her hips. He lifted her, helping her to her knees, then moved to his knees as well. Placing one hand at the small of her back, he moved the other to linger on her ribcage and his thumb stroked the beginning swell of her breast. He pressed his lips to her chin.

Abby's head lolled back as Kir slowly kissed the length of her neck, dipping in the hollows of her collarbone, and skimming the sensitive skin between her breasts. She arched, pressing her chest forward. He answered her silent request by cupping her breast and guiding the taut nipple into his warm mouth. With his tongue he lavished her bud then bit down, hard.

"*Ahhh…*" Abby couldn't help the cry that tore from her mouth as fire raced through her breast, tugging at the invisible strings attached to her womb. "Now…" She trembled. "Take me now."

Their bodies moved and rolled so that she was on her back and he was pressing her deep into the bedding with his weight.

He slid his length along hers and he wedged himself between her thighs. He groaned. "I think I've waited too long."

With one thrust he buried himself deep within her heat.

Heaven could not have felt better.

Abby's body tensed and she bowed her back. Her vaginal muscles clenched tight around his hard member. Pre-orgasmic spasms burst throughout her body, raining her with fire and ice, hot and cold, colors and emotions. The friction of their skin sliding against one another was unreal. She almost expected to see flames spark from between their heated bodies.

Instead, Kir thrust harder, faster, deeper.

Abby slowed her breathing, needing to revel in the space between pleasure and completion. Kir's breathing was heavy as he fought the inevitable, hanging on the threshold. Then he plunged forward, struck the sensitive spot deep inside Abby that broke her control. She screamed just before Kir joined her in release, plunging them both over the edge of ecstasy.

Her body shuddered with climax after climax as Kir throbbed deep inside her. Neither of them could move for a long moment. He braced himself above her, his arms to either side of her face, his cock still within her.

When the aftermath began to subside, Kir rolled from atop Abby. He brought her to her side to face him for a long, drawn-out kiss, before placing her upon her back. Using his thigh he pinned her to the bed, as if he feared she would run away again. Instead Abby curled into him, sliding her thigh between his.

The action made him smile.

With light fingertips he traced the curve of her breast and then the other. "Can you be happy, Abby—with me— here in Oz?" Before she could answer he added, "You have the freedom to choose. You may go home if it is your wish, but it is my hope that you will stay with me."

A tingling sensation rushed through Abby. Kir was offering her freedom. From the worried look on his face, she knew that offer was a huge sacrifice.

She remembered once hearing a quote that went something like, *If you love something, set it free. If it comes back, it's yours. If it doesn't, it never was.*

Was that what Kir was doing? Setting her free to see if she would return? Was it a test of her love? And most importantly, now that she'd fallen in love with Kir, could she even live without him?

Abby stroked his cheek with her palm. "Balin said my aunt is ill. She's alone, Kir. She has no one but me." She felt him tense beneath her touch when she mentioned his nemesis.

"Balin lied." Kir's expression darkened. "He is dangerous. An evil sorcerer."

Abby moved her palm along Kir's tense jaw, feeling his stubble beneath her fingertips. "But why did he want me?"

"To destroy me. To destroy the Tarok Kings. He means to rule all the lands."

Abby let her hand drop away from Kir's face. "He told me he would help me go home."

"Then it is your desire to return to Kanzaz." The strange way Kir said Kansas made Abby want to giggle, but the anguish on his face suffocated the urge.

"No—yes. I don't know. I just don't know." Abby fought the emotion crashing against the back of her eyelids. She would not cry.

"Would it be enough to verify your aunt's condition, without traveling back to Kanzaz?"

Again she struggled with the answer. Even if she discovered that Balin had lied, that Aunt Maye was well, she had not said goodbye, had not been able to tell Aunt Maye that she was unharmed when the tornado struck.

"You wish to see her, do you not?"

"Kir, she must be going out of her mind with worry. The tornado hit so quickly, things happened so fast." Abby's pulse was racing. How could she leave Kir? How could she not?

He untwined their naked limbs, pushed from the bed and rose. With a blink of an eye he donned black leather breeches. His footsteps appeared leaden as he made his way to a cabinet. The wooden doors creaked as he opened it, reached inside and drew a bundle out.

Her clothes. The things she wore when she first landed in this strange world were in his hands. He turned and held them out to her. When she made no move to come to him, he laid the clothing on a table.

Their eyes never met.

Still looking away from her, he said, "Get dressed," before pivoting and walking toward the door. He hesitated briefly before the portal. His shoulders rose sharply and trembled as they fell before he pushed the door open and walked through it.

When door swung closed, Abby felt her heart drop to the pit of her stomach. What was she supposed to do now?

Chapter Twenty-Two

ဢ

The anguish Kir felt was unlike anything he had ever experienced before. The black leather breeches he wore were suffocating. Even his skin felt foreign and too tight. A deep twisting sensation in his heart and soul made him want to lash out, to beat his fists upon anything in his path.

This sense of loss was alien to him.

He had never known love could be so joyful. So painful.

His footsteps carried him away from his bedchamber to the large cavern. He raked his hand through his wild mane, not knowing what to do next. He had never been indecisive. Had never felt so lost.

When he reached the cavern, his eyes widened in surprise as a white tiger paced the smooth rock floor toward him. He recognized her instantly from her markings and from her scent. The sorceress Kalina, who had been released from the service of the Tarok Kings only months ago, had returned.

Her steps were light, her head tilted proudly. She no longer wore any of the kings' collars around her neck. She no longer belonged to any man.

She began shapeshifting when she reached him, her white coat melting away, her limbs changing, elongating, until she stood on two legs. Her graceful arms were at her sides, her black hair flowing freely over her naked shoulders to her bare breasts, and her amber eyes lit with the fire of freedom she had so recently experienced.

She gave Kir a respectful bow of her head then tipped her face up to meet his gaze. "It is a pleasure to see you again, Lord Kir."

Despite the continuing ache in his heart for Abby, he offered Kalina the semblance of a smile. "It is good to see you are well." He paused before asking about his captain and close friend, as well as the Tarok Kings' sister. "Rafe and Mikaela? How do they fare?"

Kalina pursed her lips. Hesitated. Finally she said, "They will find their way."

Kir simply nodded his acceptance of her answer. Rafe and Mikaela were strong. They would each find a way to survive.

The sorceress held out her hand and a smooth, round ruby appeared in her palm. It was clear and a deep red, about the size of her fist. "I have seen that you and your woman have need of my services."

At that, Kir clenched his teeth. He forced himself to relax as he spoke to the sorceress who was known to be a great seer. "The woman desires to go to her home in Kanzaz." Kir tried to hold back the bitterness that rose like acid at the back of his throat.

He sensed Abby's tentative approach behind him even before he heard the click of O's toenails against the stone floor. He tensed, waiting for the moment she would reach him.

Kalina waited patiently until Abby joined them. Kir swallowed hard when he saw that his kitten was wearing the same clothing she had arrived in when she first landed in his realm, what seemed like so long ago. They were clean and mended.

The sorceress inclined her head. "You have need of transport to your home."

From the corner of his eye Kir saw the look of surprise upon Abby's features. Did he see misery in her expression as well? O settled on his haunches, looking expectantly at Kalina, as if understanding every word she spoke.

Abby raised her chin and didn't look at Kir. "Yes," was all she said.

Kalina held up the round ruby stone in her hand. It gave a soft glow that pulsed with the beat of the blood rushing through Kir's veins. "Then you must come with me," Kalina said.

Kir felt his heart would surely burst but he said nothing. Abby fidgeted with O's leash and kept her gaze averted from Kir's. Kalina waited with a calm expression, so calm that he wanted to shout at her. How could she take Abby away from him so easily? Why did the sorceress choose now to return to the known realms?

Finally Abby nodded. "Yes. Okay. Take me wherever I need to go."

Kalina returned her nod and pivoted away. They followed the sorceress through the golden doors and out into the sunshine. Abby lagged behind, drawing O along with her. The party was silent, not one of them saying a word.

Normally Kir would have reveled in the sunshine. In the sweet scents of starflowers in bloom and the smell of *ch'tok* trees. And especially Abby's unique perfume of woman.

But on this day he did not enjoy any of this. No. He wished for rain and darkness, anything that would match his torn and bitter mood. He would like nothing better than to have a sword in his hand, to be battling Balin and his *bakirs* single-handedly.

And that bastard John Steele, who was still nowhere to be found.

They followed the sorceress down the Yellow Road to the location of the red beast, the *automobile* in which Abby had arrived.

When they stopped before it, Kir's wounded gaze met Abby's cinnamon eyes, and the sorrow in them seemed to match his own. "Will you not change your mind?" he said before he could stop himself.

Abby visibly swallowed. "I—I can't. It wouldn't be right to let Aunt Maye think I'm dead. To not make sure she's all right."

His jaw tightened. He braced himself for the inevitable. "Very well," he said in a tone so sharp that Abby flinched and Kalina glanced at him.

The time had come.

Kir's gut clenched.

When the sorceress turned to Abby, the ruby lay on Kalina's outstretched palm. "Stand beside the red beast," the sorceress ordered.

This time Abby did glance at Kir. He kept his features stern and did not soften at her miserable expression. She tugged at O's leash but the dog seemed determined to stay. He planted himself on the grass and wouldn't budge. But when Abby said, "Neuter," in a low growl, Kir winced and the dog bounded toward her in a flash.

Kalina held the ruby up and it glowed so brightly that Kir almost shielded his eyes. A great wind began swirling in the meadow, glittering with red sparkles. Abby's hair floated around her shoulders and away from her fae features, but the wind seemed gentle at best.

"Goodbye, Kir." Tears rolled down Abby's cheeks. "I love you."

He nearly dropped to his knees and begged her to stay. He wanted to do that, almost needed to do that—but he couldn't. He was Lord of Oz, and he had to stand fast. Damn it. He had to save something of himself—even if it meant giving her a picture of indifference, letting her see a statue of cold marble.

Kalina moved forward, into the sparkling wind, and clenched her fists around one of Abby's hands. "Travel well," she said aloud, then murmured something softer that Kir could not hear.

It mattered not. Abby was leaving, and he would never love another.

Kalina stepped away and the wind grew in intensity, whipping Abby's hair around her face and ruffling O's fur. Then Abby, O and even the car began to sparkle. To fade in and out, their forms barely visible.

For one last moment Kir's gaze held Abby's.

The glittering wind vanished.

And with it, Kir's one and only love.

Chapter Twenty-Three

ഌ

What a head rush.

Blood surged to Abby's brain, blurring her vision and creating a churning in her stomach like the agitation of a washing machine. She braved a step, then swayed in an attempt to gain her bearings. Her muscles refused her. She collapsed against her battered Mustang and struggled to breathe.

In disbelief, her trembling palms cradled her cheeks. One minute she was in Oz, the next standing before her farmhouse in Attica, Kansas. For a moment she wondered if the events of the past month or so were just a dream. But when she felt the bulge in her pocket, she remembered the stone the beautiful sorceress had shoved into her palm as the wind begin to blow. Abby had stuffed the jewel in her pocket just before the ground disappeared from beneath her feet.

All around Abby was evidence that life had gone on in this small community without her. Even the house and barn had both survived the tornado. Bob, the old plow horse, munched happily on billowy grass in the pasture. Aunt Maye's horny rooster had a leghorn hen cornered next to the house. He dug his long spurs into the ground, his neck swaying as he mounted the hen.

This was her new reality. Kir was only a memory.

The thought closed her throat. Heat rose in her cheeks and pressure clogged her nose. Desperately, she squeezed her eyelids tight. Jaws clenched, she prayed for the strength to get past this feeling of loss, of total isolation. To forget the pain in his eyes when she left him.

O pushed his furry head beneath her palm. Whimpered. He, too, was experiencing the jet-lag effect of traveling between dimensions. And maybe missing Oz as well.

Dropping to her knees, she wrapped her arms around his neck, buried her face in his coat and released the emotion she had tried so hard to restrain. She had given up everything to make things right with Aunt Maye.

After what seemed like a lifetime, she pushed herself to her feet. Through misty eyelashes, she gazed around. Of course she'd noticed the tornado had amazingly missed the house and barn. But the chicken coop and riding arena were not as lucky. Remnants of what was left—boards, mangled tin and chicken-wire—were piled neatly where they once stood.

On wobbly legs, Abby made her way toward the stairs leading to the porch. As she grasped the handrail it swayed and she almost stumbled.

Damn, I'll have to fix that thing.

With caution she moved up the steps, then slowly walked across the porch, O at her side.

The screen door burst opened. Hand pressed against her heart, Aunt Maye stepped onto the porch. She gasped as their eyes met.

The gray-haired woman pushed out a breath and closed her eyes. Her small thin frame trembled. "Thank you, God." Then her eyes opened. "Child, where have you been?" Her voice was stern but Abby heard her concern. When her aunt frowned at O, the big coward ducked behind Abby and peeked sheepishly around her legs. Then her aunt's gaze went to the damaged Mustang.

"Lord, have mercy." She took several steps and closed the short distance between them. "Are you all right?" Her warm hands cupped Abby's biceps. The scent of yeast and mothballs flowed over Abby. Her aunt was either baking bread, or packing away old clothes, or both.

When Abby nodded, the woman pulled her into a tight embrace.

Abby stood, arms by her sides, paralyzed. Her aunt had never shown emotion. Abby heard a sniff. The woman's body trembled.

Was Aunt Maye crying? Crying for her? When her aunt's shoulders began to shake Abby wrapped her arms around the old woman.

"Don't cry. Please don't cry. I'm okay, really I am."

Maye's arms fell from around Abby. "Crying, bah." But Abby saw the woman angrily swipe at the telltale tears as she adjusted her glasses. "I haven't slept a night since you've been gone, young lady. There were stories that you tried to outrun the tornado. Balderdash, I told them. My girl is not foolish."

My girl. Aunt Maye's tenderness was surprising enough to make Abby feel like she was in the *Twilight Zone.* "Aunt Maye, are you all right? How's your heart?"

The woman wrinkled her weathered face. "Stronger than that newfangled tractor Henry bought." She tossed her hand in the direction of the big red barn. "Rest his soul." Then she smiled and Abby was afraid the woman's face might shatter as it pulled against the layer of wrinkles weighing it down. Abby couldn't remember the last time she saw Aunt Maye smile.

"Child, didn't you know only the good die young, like your uncle? Someone as ornery as your Aunt Maye will live forever." Aunt Maye's palm landed softly on Abby's ass, causing her to startle. "Now get yourself into the house and tell me what you've been about."

Abby hadn't expected this homecoming. She had been prepared to find her aunt bedridden and dying, or madder than a wet hen and ready to rake Abby over the coals for her disappearance. If she thought Oz was bizarre, returning to this new and softer Aunt Maye was scary.

As the screen door slammed behind Abby, she caught the scent of fresh baked bread filling the room. The lemon oil and camphor smells that lingered were familiar but she couldn't put her finger on something that bothered her. And then she realized what it was—the farmhouse no longer felt like home.

Home. Wasn't home where the heart was? If so Abby had no doubt where she had left her heart.

Aunt Maye settled into her favorite rocking chair. After sinking into its comfortable cushion, she said, "Sit—sit." Gray, aging eyes pinned Abby with a steely glare, a glare that had previously put the fear of God into her. "Now, child, explain where you've been."

Abby sat upon the worn flowery couch. Fast on her feet when it came to coming up with a story, Abby spun a tale of being lifted by the tornado and carried miles away. A nice elderly couple took her and O in and graciously nursed them back to health. When Abby was capable she returned home. End of story.

Maye rocked her chair, slowly and steadily. With an intense expression she listened to Abby's fable. When Abby became quiet, the rocking halted. Once more, she nailed Abby with that glare, and then a bushy brow rose.

"Gibberish!" The old woman began to rock again. "What's his name?"

Abby's eyes widened in surprise.

What was she supposed to say now?

Her mouth opened and closed. The sudden tightness in her throat squeezed off her words. Unable to talk, unable to come up with some snappy explanation, she did the only thing to do. She broke down and cried.

With strained effort, the woman rose and wobbled to Abby's side. Aunt Maye settled on the couch next to Abby and slipped her arm around Abby's shoulders. "Now, now, child. It can't be all that bad."

It felt funny to be the recipient of Aunt Maye's unfamiliar compassion. Still it felt comforting too. Abby had dreamed of this scene, or something like it, so many times. Yet now all she truly wanted were Kir's arms around her.

"So what is this fellow's name?" When Aunt Maye wanted to know something she was like a dog with a bone, so it was easier to just confess.

"Kir," Abby choked between sniffles.

"Cur! As in mongrel? Mutt?"

Abby couldn't help the chuckle that broke through her tears. "No, not C-U-R, K-I-R." In truth her aunt wasn't very far off. Kir was a wolf, after all.

Aunt Maye huffed. "What kind of name is that?"

The name of a man who held her tenderly and made passionate love to her all night long—um, after spanking her and tying her up and all kinds of other things she'd enjoyed.

The name of the man who had professed his love.

The name of an incredible man who was forever lost to Abby.

Aunt Maye released Abby, then leaned back. Her brows furrowed in thought. She cleared her throat, the hoarse rattle reminding Abby of her aunt's health. "Abby, there are things that must be said. I know you were leaving the day of the tornado. I saw your room."

So the woman had thought Abby abandoned her. "Aunt Maye—"

Aunt Maye's withered hand rose, halting Abby's words. "No, I need to say this. I haven't always treated you kindly." The old woman tapped the toe of one foot, her black thick-soled shoe patting against the wood. "I'm sorry." She pushed away from the couch as she rose. "There, I've said it. No need to bring the subject up again." She limped across the floor towards the kitchen. Before she disappeared from sight she called over her shoulder, "Now wash up for supper."

Bewildered, Abby got to her feet. The large stone in her pocket bit into her hip. Had her aunt apologized for not being exactly kind to Abby all these ears? Did this mean things would change between them in the future? And why had it taken such a horrible sacrifice for this to occur?

O scratched at the door then glanced at her expectantly. She opened the screen door and followed the dog outside. When Abby reached the Mustang, she popped the trunk and reached for her duffle bag. She needed a bath and a change of clothing before dinner.

* * * * *

Two days had passed since Abby's return to Attica. The wind had picked up, tearing at her braid and clothing as she drove the tractor into the barn. Little swirls of air played in the loose straw, stirring the golden pieces and dancing them about.

With a jolt the tractor came to a halt. Abby swung her leg over the side and jumped, jarring her teeth as her feet landed hard upon the ground. For a moment she just stood there. A light breeze skimmed her arms that were dampened with perspiration. A chill raced up her spine.

Both days she'd gone through her chores as if programmed. A listless robot. Life held no allure. She wanted or needed nothing but to wile away the hours until nighttime. Only then could she escape into a world that held desire and love—in her dreams.

All she could think of was Kir. Not just the incredible sex, but the way they had talked, how he had asked questions about her life, caring about what she thought and what she had to say.

And how he had finally offered her choice and freedom.

What kind of choice had she made?

The man who owned her heart and soul…gone.

Aunt Maye was attentive. She had hired Joey and two other young boys in Abby's absence. Even though Abby had returned, Maye had continued to employ the boys to ensure Abby's workload was lessened. Things should have been okay, but they weren't in the slightest.

Unconsciously, Abby began to move toward the barn doors. With a huff she heaved them together and secured the lock before she wandered in the direction of the house. Dusk was crawling over the horizon. It would be dark in minutes.

The sound of her boots climbing up the stairs and clunking across the porch echoed in her ears. In the distance O barked. As if all energy had left her, she sank down into the porch swing and blindly stared toward the graying sky.

The swing's sharp movement as Maye sat beside Abby startled her from her daze. She hadn't even heard her aunt's approach.

Aunt Maye placed her hand upon Abby's denim-clad knee. The strap of Abby's overalls fell past her shoulder. She brushed it back in place.

"Abby, it's time for you to go."

Abby blinked hard. "Excuse me?"

Her aunt's eyes softened. "Dear, obviously you grieve for this man. And it's time you spread your wings, find your way in life. Farming is not for you." She squeezed Abby's knee. "It never has been."

Aunt Maye's empathy was overwhelming. The woman was giving Abby the key to her prison door.

The flutter in Abby's chest died quickly. "I can't go back to him. I don't know how."

Aunt Maye patted Abby's knee as she rose. "A willing heart will find a way."

Abby's back stiffened. "That's exactly what the sorceress said."

Confusion furrowed the lines on Maye's forehead. "What?"

"A willing heart will find a way," repeated Abby.

The old woman gave a slow nod. "If your love is strong, it will lead you to your heart's desire."

Abby leaped from the swing and embraced Maye. She pressed her lips to her aunt's cheek. "Thank you," she whispered before stepping away.

A muscle ticked in Maye's neck. "When will you leave?"

"I don't know, but it will be sudden." From the things Abby knew about Oz everything happened rather unexpectedly. "I probably won't have time to say good-bye."

"Will you write?"

"I'll try," Abby promised. The skepticism on her aunt's face told Abby her aunt understood she might never see her niece again. "Aunt Maye, I love you." She threw her arms around the woman.

Her hug was returned. "I love you too, Abby." The woman tore herself from Abby's arms. She rubbed her palms on her apron. "Don't forget to take that worthless mutt. I can't and won't be responsible for the animal," her aunt called out as she opened the screen door and disappeared inside the house.

Abby took a final look around. There was something magical about the ruby the sorceress had given her. The woman had given Abby the key to return to Oz. And like an idiot, she had ignored the signs.

Duh. Kalina had used the stone to return Abby to Kansas. It was only natural that Abby could use it to return to Oz.

Wasn't it?

Abby's heart pounded as she rushed into the house. The old wood floor creaked beneath her feet as she almost skipped up the stairs.

She was going home. Home was Oz—or any place Kir was.

As Abby entered her bedroom, her train wreck appearance was reflected in the mirror. Her overalls were dirty. Her shirt splotched with things she really didn't want to think about. The scent of farm life filled her nostrils, and for the first time she didn't mind the pungent smells of manure, dirt and sweat. There were lessons in life. Growing up on a farm, yearning for love, and all the other things she had experienced, were only stair steps leading her to Kir. Her final destination would be well worth the journey.

Moving like a cyclone, she pulled off one boot and then another, tossing them in the exact place she had only a month ago. Her clothes soon followed as she hurried to the shower and turned it on.

Without waiting for the temperature to warm she stepped inside. The icy spray made her cringe, causing tiny goose bumps to rise across her naked skin. She squirted liquid soap in her palm and then began to quickly wash her abdomen. The thought of Kir's hands roaming over her body sent a flutter, like soft butterfly wings, between her thighs. Her nipples peaked, her breasts grew heavy. Fulfillment would have to wait—she was going home.

When her shower was complete, she moved toward the closet, briskly rubbing the towel across her damp hair. Abby wanted something special to wear, something sexy and easy to remove when she met Kir once again. Wire-hangers scraped across the wooden pole until she reached a spaghetti-strapped summer dress of pale blue. Tossing the towel aside, she shimmied into the soft material. Like a second skin the dress formed to her curves, stopping midway between her thighs and knees. She slipped her feet into matching sandals and then moved to the bureau.

The scent of vanilla filled the room as she quickly rubbed lotion into her elbows, arms and hands. After combing her hair, she reached beneath her pillow and extracted the ruby.

Her ticket home.

She ran through the open door, bounding down the stairs.

Midway down, Abby came to an abrupt stop. Her aunt stood at the bottom stair.

"This is it?" The woman's voice cracked.

Abby couldn't help the smile that touched her lips. Still, a tug of regret pulled at her heartstrings. The two of them had finally reached an agreement and now it was time to leave.

"Thank you." She took the last five steps slowly. Then Abby took her aunt into her arms. "Thank you for everything you've done for me. I love you." The last was said upon a whisper as they drifted apart.

"Take care, child." Aunt Maye pinched her nose and blinked hard. Without saying another word she turned and hobbled into the family room.

This *was* it, thought Abby, heading outside into the night. She let the screen door slam behind her. As she moved across the porch she grabbed the leash off the swing. Then she tucked her little fingers into the corners of her mouth and blew. A high shrill whistle had O loping down the dirt road within moments.

"Time to go, buddy." Abby snapped the leash to O's collar. He wagged his tail expectantly as if he understood each word.

Pulling O close to her side, Abby hurried down the stairs with the newly fixed rail, to a wide open space. If a tornado was going to touch down and rip them from the ground, she certainly didn't want anything harmed. She dropped O's leash, placing her foot on the leather to keep the dog in place. Then as the sorceress had done, with outstretched hands Abby held the ruby up to the blue-gray night sky. A smattering of stars twinkled above. She waited for the stone to glow, but its blood-red sheen remained the same. No bright lights or glittering red sparkles appeared.

Nothing.

Abby's heart fell.

She brought her arms down, but once again, this time with force and determination, she plunged her arms heavenward, the jewel cradled in her open palms.

Nothing.

Crestfallen, she lowered her arms. "I guess it's not to be, O." The pressure of disappointment weighted her chest. So much so that she brought her hands to her breasts, close to her heart. The minute she did, the ruby began to glow, the light growing with such intensity that Abby had to close her eyes. A wisp of a breeze swirled around her ankles, building in strength as it wrapped around her. Tiny objects stung her legs, pelting her skin like rocks and debris being tossed about. The air grew heavy, thickening, enveloping her, moving with a force that pressed against her like a cocoon.

For a moment she couldn't breathe. Night sounds, crickets chirping and doves cooing, dulled until they vanished altogether. Even O's whimper seemed muffled, far away. Then the wind died down, the air thinned. She pulled in a ragged breath—and felt rain pattering softly on her face.

Abby was afraid to open her eyes. Afraid that once she did, Kansas would be what greeted her. When O barked and pulled against his leash, Abby took a peek.

Beneath her feet were the smooth bricks of the Yellow Road glittering in the soft fall of rain. She had never been so thrilled to see the golden pathway that led to Emerald City, and more importantly, to Kir.

Finally Abby was home.

Chapter Twenty-Four

൞

Kir didn't know how lonely his existence had been until Abby left him. Before she had appeared, he'd thought his life was complete. That he needed nothing except to choose a packmate to submit to him and to bear his pups.

But Abby…

He raked his hand through his thick hair. "Enough," he growled aloud, startling a couple passing him in the emerald cavern. Without regard to them, he slowly shifted into a wolf, until he was on all fours, and strode toward the golden doors. A mere thought and the gate opened to him. The guards wisely kept their distance and their mouths shut, not daring to ask him where he was headed this day.

It had been raining the past two days since Abby had gone, matching his mood to perfection. It was dark gray outside as it continued to drizzle, the water rolling off his coat as he loped along the Yellow Road. He didn't know where he was going, he simply knew that he had to get out of Emerald City. He had to get away from memories of Abby in his bed, in his life.

Then why was he headed down the Yellow Road?

It would only bring back more memories of her, memories he wanted to wash away like the rain. In the small meadow ahead was where he had found her. The same meadow where she had left him with the aid of the sorceress' red ruby.

Perhaps Kir needed to see the place one last time in order to banish the memory of her forever.

As he loped through the forest, the clean smell of rain, pine and *ch'tok* trees met his nose. But Kir could think only about Abby's sweet scent of woman and the vanilla perfume she had worn when he first found her. His memory of it was so strong that he could almost smell it now. He shook his head, scattering droplets of rain from his muzzle. It was as if he could scent her this very moment, as if his senses were playing tricks on him.

But the closer he came to the meadow, the stronger the scent became. Did her sweet perfume still linger as if to taunt him?

His pace quickened, and he bounded through the forest as if possessed. When he reached the treeline and the small meadow where he had found and lost her, he came to a complete stop.

A woman and a dog stood in the rain, the scattering of red sparkles surrounding them slowly fading away.

Kir's heart beat so fast he could scarcely breathe. The woman's hair was slowly becoming drenched by the rain. When she pushed the locks from her face, he could clearly see her features. Clearly see the sprinkling of faerie kisses across her nose.

She dropped the sorceress' ruby stone from her hand and it rolled into the rain-soaked grass. They stood and looked at one another for a long moment. Even O remained still at her side. Then Kir began to shift into a man, rising up to his full height, completely bare of all clothing, and Abby started running to him.

Her long auburn hair swung around her shoulders, damp from the rain. Her shoes splashed in the puddles, and her thin dress clung to her curves, the material quickly turning sheer from the rain. O ran beside her.

Kir could only stand. He felt as if he was dreaming.

When she finally reached him, Abby flung herself against him, wrapping her arms around his neck and her legs around his waist. Before he had a chance to catch his breath, she pressed her lips to his in a demanding kiss that he returned with the same fervor as hers.

Gods, her taste, her smell.

Was this a dream?

No. It was truly Abby in his arms!

He finally drew away, his heart near to bursting. "You returned," was all he could think to say.

"For good." Abby's smile was so radiant it took his breath away. "I love you, Kir. I don't want to ever be away from you again."

Kir's heart nearly stopped beating. "You will be my packmate?"

She moved one hand to his cheek. "As long as I'm not caged, as long as I have my freedom, then I'm yours." She gave an impish grin. "You can tie me up and spank me as much as you and I want to in the bedroom, whenever we have sex, but outside of that I want to be your equal."

He didn't even have to stop to consider his words. "I will give you anything, anything at all, Abby. I love you, and you will always be my equal, my Alpha female."

She laughed and gave him a hard kiss. When she drew back, her voice was husky and her eyes dark with desire when she said, "But if you want to punish me for being a bad girl, I understand, M'Lord."

He cocked an eyebrow at her.

She ran her finger down his bare chest. "For leaving you to begin with, I know I deserve a spanking."

Kir's cock stirred and he gave her a playful, but reproachful look. "That you do, kitten. A punishment that should be dealt with as soon as possible."

Even though she tried to look contrite, a mischievous look sparked in her eyes. "Maybe you'd better do it now, before we get to Emerald City."

Lust raged through Kir, along with the love he felt for her. He let her slide down his length, feeling every inch of her pass over him in her slick wet dress. Rain continued to pour around them and they were both completely soaked.

When Abby was on her feet, she shot a look to O. "You get on back to Emerald City now," Abby ordered.

O whined and thumped his tail, but remained rooted to the spot.

Abby lowered her face closer to his. "I can always neuter you, boy."

The Irish wolfhound took off like a shot across the meadow, down the Yellow Road and into the forest toward Emerald City.

She looked back up at Kir and smiled. "Now where were we?"

"Have you forgotten already, wench?" Kir gave her a mock frown. "That earns you a second punishment."

Abby licked her lips and dropped her gaze. "Yes, M'Lord."

"No. Look at me." When she raised her eyes to meet his, he said, "Never lower your gaze around me, no matter what roles we play."

She clasped her hands in front of her and kept her beautiful cinnamon eyes focused on him. "Yes, M'Lord."

His cock was so painfully hard he wanted to rip that see-through dress from her body and drive into her heat. But he forced himself to retain his stern expression and go along with her wish to submit to him. It excited him in unimaginable ways to know that she still wished to surrender to him when they enjoyed one another's bodies. When they made love.

Kir pulled the top of Abby's thin dress down below her breasts, causing them to thrust up and out. She shivered and Kir groaned. He reached out and pinched each nipple between his thumb and forefinger. Abby gasped and then moaned, eyelashes fluttering as if she couldn't keep them open.

"Look at me," he demanded. As she did, he grasped her bare, wet shoulders and pushed her down so that she was on her knees. "Suck my cock, wench. And never take your eyes from mine."

His body was slick from the cool rain and when Abby's warm mouth slid over his erection, he nearly came at once. "Your punishment is to deny your own pleasure while satisfying mine," he said, knowing that it would only excite her further. "You may not touch yourself or climax without my permission."

Abby's answer was to swirl her tongue around his cock and to work its length with one of her hands, moving in tandem with the up-and-down motion of her head. Kir grasped her rain-wet hair and thrust his hips in her face, fucking her mouth like he wanted to drive inside her core.

Just when he came to the edge of climaxing, he shouted, "Stop, wench."

"What would you have me do now, M'Lord?" she asked contritely when she pulled away from him.

Kir growled his satisfaction. "On your hands and knees."

She kicked off her shoes and obeyed. He knelt behind her and pushed her dress up, baring her naked ass. He was so, so close to thrusting into her, but he stayed himself. "Do you know why you are being punished, wench?"

"For leaving you, M'Lord." Her voice came out in a breathless tone. "I promise never to leave you again."

"Nevertheless, you must be punished." He took the palm of his hand and swatted Abby's wet ass.

She cried out and he rubbed the spot, knowing he was bringing her pleasure after the sting of the slap. He smacked her ass again, and again she cried out. He repeated his motions, swatting her with his hand in a different place each time and then rubbing it with his palm.

As he spanked her, he thrust three fingers up Abby's quim with his other hand, and she began rocking into his swats and against his fingers. She lowered herself so that her head was resting on her forearms, her breasts swaying against the wet grass with every slap of his hand. He loved the bright shade of pink her ass was turning, and the way she squirmed, telling him she was on the verge of orgasm.

"May I come, M'Lord?" she begged.

"No." He kept his tone low and commanding. "You have been a very bad girl and you must be taught a lesson."

He moved away from Abby to lie down on the grass beside her. "Straddle my face."

She rose up and moved over so that she was on her hands and knees, her pussy positioned over Kir's mouth, her wet dress still around her waist. He grabbed her ass and began sucking and licking her clit and her folds. "Gods, you taste so good," he said in between licks.

Abby squirmed even more. "I'm so close, M'Lord. May I come now?"

"You have not been suitably punished." He licked her harder, his tongue driving inside her core.

Abby's wet thighs trembled so hard in his grip he knew it was taking everything she had not to climax.

He pulled her downward from his face to his waist so that she was sitting on his cock, with him still lying on the wet grass. "I want you to ride me. And ride me hard."

"Yes, M'Lord," she said with a look of satisfaction on her face, showing her obvious pleasure at his instructions.

Abby rose up on her knees while he positioned his cock at the entrance to her channel. She slowly came down on his erection, a look of incredible pleasure on her face as she completely took him inside her.

Kir could only groan as he looked up at her, as he felt himself inside her. She began riding him, keeping a slow, rhythmic pace as the rain continued to pour upon them. She pushed her wet hair away from her fae features, and the sprinkling of faerie kisses on her nose and shoulders took his breath away.

She yanked her dress from around her waist, over her head, and tossed it aside on the grass so that her beautiful body was bared completely to him.

"Ride me harder," he said as he grabbed her hips and began forcibly moving her faster and faster on his cock. "Touch your breasts."

Without hesitation, Abby cupped her breasts in her hands and began pinching and pulling her own nipples as they fucked one another harder and faster in the shower of cool water pouring from the sky. Her eyes were nearly rolling back in her head and she was obviously close to climax.

His orgasm wouldn't wait much longer either.

Several more thrusts, wet flesh slapping wet flesh, their moans and groans filling the air.

He shouted, "Come, kitten!"

Abby shouted, her face tipped to the sky, rain rolling down her features. She continued riding him, her channel clenching and unclenching around his cock.

With his own shout, Kir came in a rush. His seed filled Abby as she still rode him, drawing out all of his come until he couldn't handle anymore.

"Enough." He rolled them both over so that they were side-by-side on the soft grass, looking into one another's eyes. His cock was still buried in her core and her channel continued to spasm around him.

When at last their breathing had slowed, Kir finally found the breath to say, "I love you, Abby."

She smiled and brushed her lips over his. "And I love you, my wolf-man."

Chapter Twenty-Five

ॐ

Warm water swirled around her body and a jaunty breeze feathered Abby's hair about her face and shoulders as she gazed across the rolling ocean. Blue-green waves swelled, then broke, cresting with white frothy foam. Her nipples beaded under the currents caressing her breasts, her naked body, like tiny sensual fingertips dancing upon her skin. Every nerve ending tingled with anticipation.

Yesterday she had come back to Oz. Today she would wed the man of her dreams. A smile touched her lips with the remembrance of her and Kir's first meeting. She had thought him a figment of her imagination—the perfect dream—the perfect man.

Her shoulders rose and settled on a heavy sigh.

A gust of wind off the northern mountains chilled her exposed skin. Abby crossed her arms over her chest and ran her hands briskly along her arms. The weather was changing in Oz.

"M'Lady." Abby turned to see Linara rise from a deep bow. Beside her stood Kalina. "It is time." The healer's dark gaze scanned Abby's body with appreciation. Heat fanned Abby's face as she averted her eyes to Kalina.

A hint of a smile touched Kalina's full lips. "As it was meant to be."

The exchange between the two women was broken as Linara spoke, "Lord Kir would not be pleased should you take ill." Linara curled her fingers, long, red fingernails waving Abby forward. "Please come inside and allow me to prepare you for the ceremony."

Abby moved from out of the warmth of the water into the chill of the air. While they began to walk toward Emerald City, a hint of unease stirred within her as she wondered what preparations the healer was talking about. Then as quickly as the anxiety rose, it died. Abby would soon be the Mistress of Oz and she might as well begin by expressing her likes and dislikes now. Starting with all this mystery shit. If she still wanted to know what was happening when they reached their destination, she would damn well ask.

As they neared the masked entrance to the caves, the earth opened. Flowers and rich vegetation parted like a curtain, allowing the three women to enter, then closed silently behind them.

Excitement reigned throughout the brightly lit halls. Each time one of Kir's subjects rushed by, they paused, bowed and gifted Abby with a broad smile before continuing on their way. She felt their joy. Sensed their approved in their Master's choice of packmate.

Abby was ushered through halls and finally towards a room adjacent to Kir's. When the door swung wide, she gasped.

The chamber was beautiful.

A canopy bed with rich green silk draped along the railings was off to her right. To the left was a full-size mirror and a dressing table, its top littered with trinkets, lotions, oils and jewels. Instead of a shower masked by a wall, it flowed freely. The light cascade was pleasing to her eyes and ears, as the vast array of flowers was to her nose.

Linara walked in between two armoires and waved her hand in front of the rock wall. The solid barrier blurred and then, inch by inch, formed into an archway leading into the next room. The masculine sound of Kir's laughter made Abby take a step forward, his voice drawing her like a lodestone. Quickly the healer lowered her arm and the passage disappeared. "I believe it is one of your practices that the groom and bride be separated until just before the union?"

Abby was touched that the woman had researched some of her native customs.

Yet when Abby met the healer's gaze, the woman's dark pupils dilated and Abby could see the lust within their depths. Abby didn't sense the woman held resentment. Still, she knew Linara felt disappointment. After this day neither she nor any other woman would grace Kir's bed.

The Master of Oz was Abby's man—and hers alone.

Kalina steps were graceful as she floated to one of the armoires and opened it. Abby recognized some of her clothes hanging among several outfits that were not familiar. Again she was moved by Kir's thoughtfulness. He had ensured she had remnants of her old life. Even her mother and father's picture hung on the wall. Someone must have traveled back to her Kansas home and retrieved some of her belongings.

I hope they didn't give Aunt Maye a heart attack.

The thought disappeared when Kalina withdrew the most extravagant dress—and the sheerest—Abby had ever seen. The white gauze had the appearance of mist or a wispy cloud, as if you could brush your hand through it and not disturb a thread. The neckline plunged low and wide, and was laced with tiny blood-red rubies. The hem was oblique, dipping long and delicate to one side. Sleeveless, the armpits plunged low, gathering at the waist.

Abby inhaled sharply and pressed her hand to her mouth as Linara presented her with a pair of ruby slippers. Actually, they were three-inch stilettos. The heels were transparent rubies. The leather of the shoe itself was covered with crushed rubies that glistened beneath the lights. Four gold chains crisscrossed from one side to the next, four bright diamonds twinkled where they intersected and would lie upon the top of Abby's feet.

"They're beautiful," whispered Abby.

Linara set the dress upon the bed and placed the shoes next to it. "The slippers were Lord Kir's choice."

The thought that Kir had selected something so fine, so beautiful, so perfect, sent a thrill through Abby's heart.

All of this was unbelievable.

After guiding Abby to a chair in front of the dressing table, Linara began to run a comb through Abby's hair even before her ass hit the seat. Within moments the damp ends were dry and the mass was full and lustrous.

Cool air brushed the back of her neck as Linara swept Abby's heavy mane up and twirled and twisted the locks. Within minutes a waterfall of curls hung from a crown perched upon her head. Strings of diamonds and rubies were interwoven within the ringlets.

Abby stood, holding her arms high, as Kalina slipped the dress over her head. A tremor shook Abby as the material moved across her sensitive skin.

"It-it..." Abby stuttered.

"...feels like it is alive," finished Linara.

Abby nodded, biting the inside of her cheek as the dress caressed her breasts. Her nipples tightened, electricity stinging the tips.

"The cloth is a gift from Prince Eral. It is from the ocean."

Kalina's brows rose at Linara's words. Kalina normally did not betray her feelings in any way. Yet there was definitely something behind her eyes at the mention of the prince.

The sorceress knelt, placing the stilettos in front of Abby. When she slipped her feet into the slippers, chills skittered over her skin. Within minutes she would be married to Kir.

Kalina rose and with a twist of her fingers, she produced a necklace, each end held between her thumbs and forefingers. The necklace was a spider's web of the finest gold, a network of tiny chains, with a smattering of diamonds and rubies that sparkled as if fire burned inside them. It was magnificent. When the sorceress draped it across Abby's chest, each precious gem made a pinprick of heat against her skin.

"It is a gift from Lord Kir, a sign of unity," Linara said. "Werewolves have an aversion to collars." Her gaze flickered to Kalina, who'd only recently surrendered the collars of the weretiger kings to become a free woman.

Abby stroked one finger lightly, almost reverently, across the necklace. "It is an honor to wear his gift." Removing her hand, she took one last look at her reflection, hardly recognizing the woman who stared back.

There was a knock on the door. All three women turned as Prince Eral entered. He knelt on one knee, his head bowed. "M'lady, your Lord awaits you." He rose and extended his arm.

Air crackled as if with a power surge. The small hairs on Abby's arms rose as she wondered at its source. That's when she noticed Prince Eral's and Kalina's gazes had locked on one another. Dry timber wouldn't burn as hot.

"Shall we?" When Linara spoke the heaviness in the room dissipated, almost as if it had never been there.

Abby folded her arm in the crook of Eral's. Linara and Kalina quietly followed them out of the room.

The Emerald Cavern was lit with a million pinpricks of light, as if God had dropped a scattering of stars upon the room. They fell from the rocky ceiling, suspended in midair, and twinkled brightly. From deep, carved alcoves, sconces of large emeralds blazed and joined the small illuminations. A wild overgrowth of greenery and flowers crept across the stone walls.

The large hall must have contained every member of Kir's pack, as well as the entire group of Tarok Kings and their mates. Awai and Alexi stood beside their men. Two more statuesque and gorgeous men were next to them. One man had a heart tattoo on his biceps. The other man turned his back to talk to someone behind him, and Abby saw that he had a diamond tattoo on his ass, barely visible from the top of this leather pants. Both men embraced beautiful women in their arms, one who was blonde and the other dark-haired with glasses.

And beside them was Aunt Maye.

Abby almost stumbled when she saw her aunt standing amongst the half-dressed people. Hell, half of them were entirely naked. Any minute Abby expected her staunch aunt to drop to her knees and begin praying for everyone's lost soul. When her aunt smiled, Abby fought the sensation to cover herself with her arms.

Prince Eral leaned closer and whispered. "It is a gift from Lord Kir. She will not remember anything but attending her niece's wedding." Then he winked. "She believes you are being married on an island called Hawaii with all guests appropriately attired." Then he added, "You look lovely in the fashionable wedding dress your aunt chose."

Abby took a deep breath of amazement. Her aunt had chosen this creation?

Then she saw Kir and the air she'd just managed to suck in left her lungs again in a rush.

He was magnificent. The image of greatness, of nobility. White breeches made of the same transparent material as her gown graced his muscular body. Her eyes narrowed on the bulge between his thighs. Kir's throaty growl brought her gaze to his. Hot, carnal lust burned in the depths of his blue eyes.

Abby's body immediately reacted. A firestorm whipped through her veins. Moisture pooled between her legs as her breasts grew heavy with need. For two cents she'd throw caution to the wind and jump the man's bones in front of everyone.

Prince Eral placed Abby's hand in Kir's and everyone in the room disappeared. No one else existed for Abby. Her reflection was in his eyes and she would soon be united with his soul.

Kir released her hand, lowered himself to his knees, and kissed each of her feet. His lips were warm, sending a ray of sunshine up her legs.

"Where you go, I will follow." His voice was coarse as sandpaper.

Then he moved his hands, curving them around her ankles and moving them slowly over her calves and knees. He pushed up the light material of her gown with his exploration until he brought his palms to her mons.

"Together we will live as one…" His gentle touch smoothed over her abdomen. "…bringing life into this world…" Her gown was bunched around her waist, but it didn't matter. Nothing mattered except for the words Kir spoke.

Then he stood, his palms moving onward, each stopping to cup her breasts. "…fed by your body and cherished by mine." Then with a swift movement he disposed of her gown. Like a feather, the dress floated in slow motion toward the floor, leaving her standing only in the ruby stilettos.

Kir cupped her face in his palms. His eyes shone with love, humbling Abby.

"With my kiss, I breathe my life into you and receive yours in exchange." His soft lips touched her gently, growing firm as his palms slid behind her neck and then began to roam.

A man cleared his throat, breaking the trance that had spun a net around Abby and Kir.

Their mouths parted. Kir took a step back, gazing at Abby expectedly.

Damn. No one had prepped her for this ceremony. She didn't know what to expect, much less what to do. When in doubt, follow the leader.

Abby dropped to her knees and kissed each of Kir's feet, paying no heed to her bare ass raised in the air. "Where you go, I will follow…"

Her fingers curled around his ankle, gently smoothing over the taut muscles of his calves. The material of his pants ripped. She gave Kir a desperate look. He nodded. When her hands reached his knees, the tearing of cloth was arousing. As she skimmed over his thighs, she couldn't help pressing her thumbs on the inside of his legs.

He raised a brow. His member jerked.

Teasing fingers wove through the golden hairs above his erection, so clearly visible through the thin material of his pants that remained. "Together we will live as one…" Her fingers curled around his cock. He growled, growing harder, firmer beneath her touch. She stroked from base to tip. Kir's head lolled back, as he inched his legs further apart.

"…bringing life into this world…" When she stood, she released Kir's erection and her gaze locked with his. Slowly, seductively, her tongue slid between her lips. Her lashes lowered. She cupped her breasts with her palms. "…fed by my body and cherished by yours…"

Then she reached for Kir's breeches, her fingers tucked into the waistband. With a swift yank, the sound of tearing material was loud as she ripped his pants from his body. As she tossed the remnants atop her gown, there were soft female giggles from the audience, joined by deep, low growls.

With a jerk, Kir brought her into his embrace. Their breathing was labored.

"With my kiss, I breathe my life into you and receive yours in exchange." She barely got the words out before his mouth found hers. There was a pull deep inside her, as if her very soul was being drawn from her body. Then a reverse force, as if Kir's soul replaced hers. Her knees weakened and Kir's grip tightened around her.

The ground began to shake. Thunder echoed in her head.

Not thunder… Applause.

When Kir released her, the room exploded with congratulations. As if caught in a tornado, she was pulled and passed from one person to another, man and woman alike, each sharing a kiss, bonding and uniting her as one of the pack.

As a man spun her around she caught a glimpse of Kir being kissed by several women. The smug look on his face stirred something inside her. The next man who held her she kissed willingly. A loud, menacing growl rent the air. The room went deathly quiet.

When a familiar hand cupped the nape of her neck, pulling her around, she faced Kir.

"That is enough. No more kissing," he bellowed.

Abby started to giggle.

"You think it's funny?" he asked.

She nodded and couldn't stop giggling.

When his firm hand met her ass, she started. Anger lit like a spark inside her until she saw the possessiveness in his eyes.

"My lips will be the only lips you kiss." Kir nuzzled his nose into her hair. His touch gentled. "Agreed, M'Lady?" he added.

"And the same goes for you, too, buster. Agreed?" Man, he was making her hot. His handprint smarted. The tender nuzzling was enough to make her want to melt in his arms.

"Agreed." With a hand beneath her knees he swept her into his arms. She grasped for his neck, gaining purchase and drawing herself tight against his chest. "Say hello and goodbye to your aunt. I cannot wait any longer to be inside you."

Aunt Maye was waiting at the door. Kir released Abby's legs and she slid down his firm length. It felt funny to be stark naked in front of her aunt, wearing only those ruby stilettos. Yet when her aunt pulled her into an embrace, seemingly unaware of Abby's lack of clothing, Abby relaxed.

"Your gentleman tells me that you must leave immediately for your honeymoon on one of the other islands." Maye held Abby a foot away from her. "He seems like a nice enough man. If you ever need to come home for a visit, there will always be a room for you."

Abby couldn't stop the single tear that slipped from her eye. "Thank you."

"Abby," Kir warned through a growl. His cock was large and hard, growing firmer beneath Abby's open scrutiny. His voice rumbled, a sound from deep within his throat. He scooped her back into his arms.

After several goodbyes they slipped away from the crowd and were finally alone. They stood before her bedchamber. Kir used mind thought to open the door and then he carried her over the threshold.

Kir's sultry gaze scanned the room as he slid her body tight against his, settling Abby upon her feet. Then a wicked smile crossed his expression. That sexy, *come here, baby, let's get it on* look that made her legs wobbly. She could hardly stand in those ruby heels.

"You were very, very bad during the ceremony." He attempted to sound gruff but the gleam in his eyes gave him away.

Abby pushed her bottom lip out. "It's your fault. You never explained the ceremony or what I was supposed to do."

"But did you have to stroke me?"

Her hand slipped between their bodies. "Like this?" she purred as her hand folded around his shaft and pumped once, twice.

His hips moved into her palm. "Yes," he hissed between clenched teeth.

"Did you prefer I do this?" She dropped to her knees and took him into her mouth, before he could stop her.

His back arched as he pushed into her warmth. "No—yes."

The play of her tongue moving up and down his length stole his breath. She heard the struggle in his breathing as his fingers began to pluck pins from her hair. As she took him deeper, her hair fell around her shoulders.

He sucked air slowly into his lungs as he gently stepped away. "I'm too close. I want you too badly."

Using his body, her hands skimming up his limbs, she stood. "Then take me, M'Lord, any...way...you...want."

She started to kick off her ruby shoes, but Kir stayed her hand. "Leave them," he said gruffly.

His mouth came hard upon hers as he drew her against him. Step by step, they moved closer to the canopy bed, never lessening their hold on one another. Abby felt the edge of the bed against the backs of her knees, and then they were tumbling, limbs intertwined, bodies melting into one another.

There would be a lifetime for slow and gentle. Tonight was for fast and hard.

Kir spread her legs wide, positioned between her thighs, and entered Abby with one thrust.

She screamed, her orgasm striking hard and fast, from out of nowhere.

His deep, penetrating thrusts only intensified the heat, the sensations. Her body was a furnace. She was burning up, ready to explode again.

As Kir's climax ripped through his body, Abby ignited. His come was molten lava gushing to every part of her womb. Everywhere it touched turned her liquid, their juices mixing, uniting.

He continued to pump in and out, in and out. His golden mane was wild as he raised his head heavenward and released a haunting howl, before ejaculating once more.

Still he continued to thrust.

Their eyes met and naked hunger reflected back, making her nipples sting, tugging on her pussy. When he bounced against her G-spot, lightning raced through her. At the same time Kir's body released, hips grinding into her mons, driving him deeper than he had ever reached.

Fireworks shattered behind Abby's eyelids. Never had she experienced anything like this. As her body began to cool, her pulse finally slowing, Kir rolled from atop her, taking her with him.

Pressed next to him, she listened to the beat of his heart, her heart pounding in rhythm.

"I love you," he murmured.

She snuggled closer. "I love you too."

"What do you think of the names Astoria, Alzandra and Akron?" His breath tickled the hairs next to her ear.

She wiggled from his embrace. "What?"

He grinned, a smile that went ear to ear. "Names. For our girls and their brother."

"Nooo…" She tried to deny what his proud expression revealed. But deep inside, she was beaming. "So that howl was for your son, while your daughters received only a grunt or two?"

His eyes widened. His jaw went slack. The look of shock on his face was priceless.

She laughed, pushing him upon his back and then straddling him, resting upon his thighs. Her fingers closed around his semi-hard phallus. She pumped from base to tip feeling him stiffen, harden. When he was fully erect, she positioned her body over his hips. Slowly, achingly slow, she slid her body over his cock, burying him deep.

His hands gripped her hips.

She gave him a mischievous grin. "Now, let's see if we can try for Alexander… Even up the numbers."

About the Authors

𝕊

Cheyenne McCray

National bestselling author Cheyenne McCray is the award-winning author of sixteen books and six novellas. Among other accolades, Chey has been presented with the prestigious Romantic Times BOOKclub's Reviewers' Choice Award for "Best Erotic Romance of the Year."

Chey has been writing ever since she can remember, back to her kindergarten days when she penned her first poem. She always knew one day she would write novels, hoping her readers would get lost in the worlds she created, as she did when she was lost in a good book. Cheyenne enjoys spending time with her husband and three sons, traveling, and of course writing, writing, writing.

Cheyenne welcome comments from readers. You can find their website and email addresses on their author bio page at www.ellorascave.com.

Also by Cheyenne McCray

❧

Blackstar: Future Knight

Castaways

Ellora's Cavemen: Tales of the Temple III *(anthology)*

Erotic Invitation

Erotic Weekend

Erotic Stranger

Erotic Interludes - collection of all three "Erotic" stories; only available in print

Hearts are Wild *(anthology)*

Seraphine Chronicles: Forbidden

Seraphine Chronicles: Bewitched

Seraphine Chronicles: Spellbound

Seraphine Chronicles: Untamed

Things That Go Bump in the Night 3 *(anthology)*

Vampire Dreams with Annie Windsor

Wildfire

Wildcat

Wildcard

Wild Borders

Wonderland: King of Hearts

Wonderland: King of Spades

Wonderland: King of Diamonds

Wonderland: King of Clubs

Mackenzie McKade

A taste of the erotic, a measure of daring, and a hint of laughter describes Mackenzie McKade's novels. She sizzles the pages with scorching sex, fantasy, and deep emotion that will touch you and keep you immersed until the end. Whether her stories are contemporaries, futuristics, or fantasies this Arizona native thrives on giving you the ultimate erotic adventure.

When not traveling through her vivid imagination she's spending time with three beautiful daughters, a devilishly handsome grandson, and the man of her dreams. She loves to write, enjoys reading, and can't wait till summer. Boating and jet-skiing are top on her list of activities. Add to that laughter and if mischief is in order-Mackenzie's your gal! Visit Mac on the web at www.mackenziemckade.com.

Mackenzie welcome comments from readers. You can find their website and email addresses on their author bio page at www.ellorascave.com.

Also by Mackenzie McKade

ഌ

A Tall Dark Cowboy
Ecstasy: The Game
Ecstasy: Forbidden Fruit
A Very Faery Christmas

Why an electronic book?

We live in the Information Age — an exciting time in the history of human civilization, in which technology rules supreme and continues to progress in leaps and bounds every minute of every day. For a multitude of reasons, more and more avid literary fans are opting to purchase e-books instead of paper books. The question from those not yet initiated into the world of electronic reading is simply: *Why?*

1. ***Price.*** An electronic title at Ellora's Cave Publishing and Cerridwen Press runs anywhere from 40% to 75% less than the cover price of the exact same title in paperback format. Why? Basic mathematics and cost. It is less expensive to publish an e-book (no paper and printing, no warehousing and shipping) than it is to publish a paperback, so the savings are passed along to the consumer.

2. ***Space.*** Running out of room in your house for your books? That is one worry you will never have with electronic books. For a low one-time cost, you can purchase a handheld device specifically designed for e-reading. Many e-readers have large, convenient screens for viewing. Better yet, hundreds of titles can be stored within your new library — on a single microchip. There are a variety of e-readers from different manufacturers. You can also read e-books on your PC or laptop computer. (Please note that Ellora's

Cave does not endorse any specific brands. You can check our websites at www.ellorascave.com or www.cerridwenpress.com for information we make available to new consumers.)

3. *Mobility*. Because your new e-library consists of only a microchip within a small, easily transportable e-reader, your entire cache of books can be taken with you wherever you go.

4. ***Personal Viewing Preferences.*** Are the words you are currently reading too small? Too large? Too... ANNOYING? Paperback books cannot be modified according to personal preferences, but e-books can.

5. ***Instant Gratification.*** Is it the middle of the night and all the bookstores near you are closed? Are you tired of waiting days, sometimes weeks, for bookstores to ship the novels you bought? Ellora's Cave Publishing sells instantaneous downloads twenty-four hours a day, seven days a week, every day of the year. Our webstore is never closed. Our e-book delivery system is 100% automated, meaning your order is filled as soon as you pay for it.

Those are a few of the top reasons why electronic books are replacing paperbacks for many avid readers.

As always, Ellora's Cave and Cerridwen Press welcome your questions and comments. We invite you to email us at Comments@ellorascave.com or write to us directly at Ellora's Cave Publishing Inc., 1056 Home Avenue, Akron, OH 44310-3502.

THE
☥ ELLORA'S CAVE ☥
LIBRARY

Stay up to date with Ellora's Cave Titles in
Print with our Quarterly Catalog.

TO RECIEVE A CATALOG,
SEND AN EMAIL WITH YOUR NAME
AND MAILING ADDRESS TO:

CATALOG@ELLORASCAVE.COM

OR SEND A LETTER OR POSTCARD
WITH YOUR MAILING ADDRESS TO:

CATALOG REQUEST
c/o ELLORA'S CAVE PUBLISHING, INC.
1056 HOME AVENUE
AKRON, OHIO 44310-3502

erridwen, the Celtic Goddess of wisdom, was the muse who brought inspiration to storytellers and those in the creative arts. Cerridwen Press encompasses the best and most innovative stories in all genres of today's fiction. Visit our site and discover the newest titles by talented authors who still get inspired - much like the ancient storytellers did, once upon a time.

ELLORA'S CAVEMEN

LEGENDARY TAILS

Try an e-book for your immediate
reading pleasure or order these titles in print from

WWW.ELLORASCAVE.COM

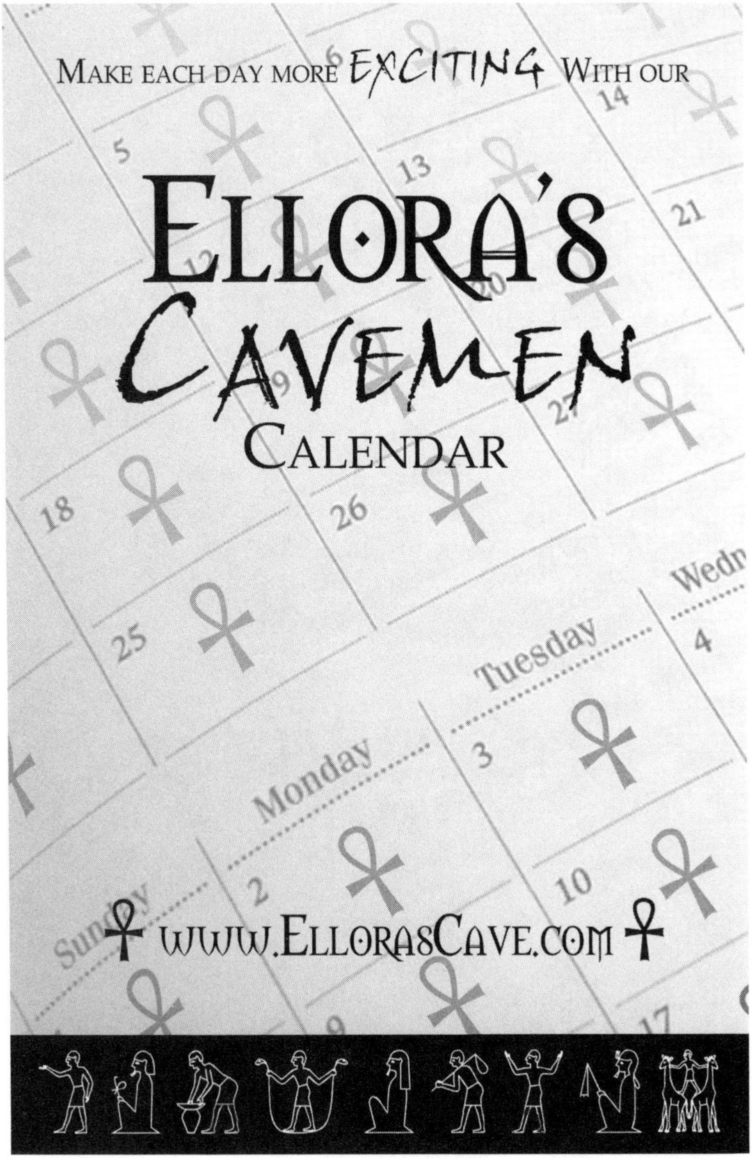
Make each day more EXCITING With our
Ellora's
Cavemen
Calendar
www.EllorasCave.com